SHADOW HOUSE

The Gathering

DAN POBLOCKI

SCHOLASTIC INC.

For Bruce

ISBN 978-1-338-25637-6

Copyright © 2016 by Scholastic Inc. All rights reserved. Published by Scholastic Inc., *Publishers since 1920.* SCHOLASTIC, SHADOW HOUSE, and associated logos are trademarks and/or registered trademarks of Scholastic Inc.

12 11 10 9 8 7 6 5 4 3 2   18 19 20 21 22 23

Printed in the U.S.A.   40

First Scholastic paperback printing, January 2018

CHAPTER 1

WHENEVER POPPY CALDWELL glanced in a mirror, she saw another girl standing behind her.

There were plenty of other girls at Thursday's Hope, the group home where Poppy had lived since age six. But the Girl wasn't like the other girls.

Poppy was pretty sure she was dead.

In the mirror, the Girl always appeared smiling, hazel eyes glinting with playful kindness, long dark hair slanting sharply across her forehead. She always wore the same white pinafore over a dark dress, with large pockets that gaped near her hips and seemed filled with mystery.

Poppy knew that seeing the Girl was odd. Was she a ghost? An angel? Once, Poppy had worked up the courage to ask her bunkmate Ashley if it was normal for girls to appear behind you in mirrors—girls who couldn't speak, girls who weren't actually in the room with you when you turned around. Ashley had laughed so hard, Poppy had forced herself to giggle too, pretending it was all a joke.

She thought she'd be able to keep her secret. But Ashley didn't like keeping secrets.

Tales of Poppy's visions spread through the dormitory like smoke, and Poppy acquired an unfortunate nickname: *Crazy Poppy*. For a while, she tried to argue, hoping that she could convince the others that the Girl was real. It only made the teasing worse.

Poppy started to believe that she actually *was* crazy.

But whenever things got really bad, when the other girls of Thursday's Hope badgered her ruthlessly, the Girl was Poppy's special comfort—a friend who made her less lonely, less afraid. Sometimes when a mirror caught her eye, Poppy would find the Girl peering back at her, and the Girl would remove an item from one of the giant pockets of her smock and then hold it up as if to make Poppy smile.

The next morning, Poppy would discover the item tucked under her pillow.

The first time, it had been a thin wire twisted into the shape of a finch. Then came pressed flowers, out-of-print comic strips snipped from yellowed newspapers, a paintbrush with dried green paint at its tip.

Old things.

Surprising things.

Strange things.

At first, Poppy couldn't believe it was happening. But the objects were there—she could hold them in her hand, and that meant they were real. Unexplainable, but real.

Poppy treasured these items, tucking them inside a book she'd hollowed out to keep them secret. But Ashley took particular pleasure in raiding Poppy's belongings, passing the Girl's treasures to the others, who would tear and sometimes destroy them. On those nights, Poppy had nightmares of terrible fires, and watched, screaming, as her bunkmates burned around her. The worst part was that in those dreams, Poppy was always the one to light the flames.

In real life, Poppy didn't know how to fight back . . . until the day Ashley got her hands on a delicate charcoal sketch of five kids in masks and uniforms, all lined up against a stone wall. Poppy had hidden the sketch in a separate place, between the pages of a book she loved, a book she knew Ashley would never, ever read. But Ashley was a better snoop than Poppy had imagined. Poppy found her standing beside their bunks, the drawing held roughly in her hands.

"Is this from your *friend*?" Ashley asked with a thin, flat smile. She tensed her hand threateningly on the sketch.

Something inside Poppy broke. Before she could stop herself, she reached for Ashley's favorite possession, an ornate mirror on their shared nightstand, and swung it. There was a smash. A scream. Ashley clutched her hand into a fist—but the sketch had already slipped away from her. Miraculously, it landed unharmed on Poppy's bed.

Poppy just watched as Ashley howled for help.

Poppy had never been sent to Ms. Tate's office before. Its cold, metal cabinets and big oak desk had always intimidated Poppy when she walked past it. Now she was seated in front of the desk, in the chair for troublemakers. The secretary told her in no uncertain terms to not touch a thing and to wait there until Ms. Tate had checked on Ashley.

Poppy knew she should listen. She was in enough trouble already. But her stomach was churning with so much anger that it burned her usual meekness away. For once, she didn't hesitate to take the chance she'd always dreamed about. As soon as the office door closed behind her, Poppy was out of her chair and searching the cabinets for her own file. If she was already in big trouble, why not get in a little more?

The room smelled too sweet, as if there was bubble gum stuck underneath every piece of furniture. Sunlight streamed in through the tall window, illuminating a dust-mote storm that swirled around Poppy as she searched. The filing cabinet stood against the far wall. Poppy found the correct drawer, removed her folder, and placed it on Ms. Tate's desk.

Pawing through the material, a veil of disappointment fell on Poppy. There were report cards and medical records, pictures she'd painted when she was much younger, but not a single thing from before she'd arrived at the group home. She'd wanted to find out about her parents, but as far as the file was concerned, her parents had never existed. Poppy had come from nowhere.

This was highly unusual.

And then it got more unusual.

Near the back of the folder, Poppy found a sealed envelope with her name on it. She turned it over again and again, almost dizzy with excitement.

In the upper-left corner, written in pen by a delicate hand, were the words *Larkspur House, Hardscrabble Road, Greencliffe, NY.* The postmark was smudged, so Poppy couldn't read the date it had been sent.

A letter? The anger flooded her again. Why had Ms. Tate never given it to her?

Poppy slid her fingernail carefully under the flap. Inside rested a slip of salmon-colored stationery with intricate floral designs lining every edge. It was one of the most beautiful objects she had ever seen. There was a small photograph of a luscious country mansion tucked in the envelope too. Placing that aside, she began to read.

My Dearest Niece,

Oh what a relief to have finally found you! You have no idea what the family has been through, though I'm sure it is nothing compared to the life you've been forced to lead. Poor thing!

You may call me Great-Aunt Delphinia. I live on a grand estate in the Hudson Valley with more room than I know what to do with. It would be such an honor if you would consider coming to stay with me. I will provide the best schooling, cuisine, and clothing—all the comforts that any girl could ever wish for— though I'm sure you understand that those things would be worthless without the loving household that will form the foundation of your new life here at Larkspur. The photograph of the grounds should provide an idea of what you are in for!

I would come down to Thursday's Hope to collect you if it weren't for my health. But please do let me know that you've received this letter, and I shall arrange for your immediate travel from the city. We've so much to discuss!

Yours truly and with love,
Delphinia Larkspur

Poppy closed her eyes as chills brushed her skin, and her eyes flooded with tears. This was better than any treasure the Girl had ever given her. It was like something out of a fairy tale, and not something that could happen to a girl like her. Family! A happy ending!

Somewhere in the office behind her, the floor creaked. Poppy whipped around to find the director standing just inside the doorway.

"And just what do you think you're doing, Miss Caldwell?" Ms. Tate glanced at the folder lying open on her desk as well as the envelope in Poppy's hands.

"I want to ask you about my file," said Poppy, trying to hide the trembling in her voice.

"That file is not meant to be seen by you," Ms. Tate chided in her best *rules-are-rules* voice.

Poppy's face burned. "I found this." She held up the envelope. "A letter. Addressed to me." She made herself look Ms. Tate in the eyes. "Why would you hide it from me?"

Ms. Tate's expression shifted from anger to confusion. "I would never! Let me see that."

Poppy handed it over reluctantly. She watched as Ms. Tate scanned the writing. "Poppy, I've never seen this before. I swear."

"I have a family!" Poppy said.

"Let's not jump to conclusions."

"My great-aunt Delphinia knows all about me." Poppy's voice was small but insistent.

Ms. Tate sighed, looking like she'd seen this sort of thing before. "The return address is vague. There's no phone number. No email. How do you expect me to even get in touch with her?"

I don't, Poppy thought. *I'll figure it out myself.*

At the look on Poppy's face, Ms. Tate rounded the desk and sat down in front of her computer. Poppy watched, barely daring to breathe, as the director searched the Internet for evidence of this Larkspur House. "I'm not getting much. Just a dozen or so real estate listings from all around the country. And I can't find a thing about a Delphinia Larkspur."

Poppy's chest collapsed in on her. "So that's it?"

"I know the girls have not been kind to you lately." Ms. Tate leaned back in her chair and gave Poppy an apologetic look.

"I think you're going to have to accept that this was a joke. And in the meantime, you still have your actions to account for. What you did to Ashley is inexcusable." Poppy was still very much in trouble.

Later that night, when Poppy approached the mirror over the sink in the bathroom, the Girl was not there.

This had never happened before.

Only after Poppy had slipped beneath her sheets, watching the reflected glow of car headlights drift across the ceiling, listening to the wheezing of Ashley on the lower bunk, did she make the connection: *Maybe now that I have the possibility of Larkspur House and Great-Aunt Delphinia, I don't need the Girl anymore.*

Poppy couldn't have been more wrong.

CHAPTER 2

MARCUS GELLER HEARD music that no one else seemed to notice, music emanating from inside a nearby room that only he was aware of.

There was no way to fight this music. No way to ignore it.

So whenever he could, Marcus tried to play along.

Marcus had just sat down on the stool in the corner of the dining room, hugging the cello between his knees and raising the bow, when his mother called out to him. "Marcus! Would you come up here, please?" Her voice sounded thin and far away, and he knew that she'd parked herself at her computer in her bedroom upstairs, her usual spot for hiding from the real world.

Marcus felt a knobby object rise up his esophagus. He hadn't even begun practicing yet today, and already his mom was preparing to stop him. He squeezed his hands into fists and then released them slowly before answering, "Can you give me a minute!" Then he drew the bow across the strings, filling the room with a deep, resonant hum that drowned out all of his worries, as well as his mother's reply.

Practicing at home had always been difficult—finding privacy when you have three older siblings living under the same roof is akin to discovering a unicorn sleeping under your bed—but recently, the problem had been even more complicated.

Marcus's music seemed to be affecting his mother in an unusual way.

His mother's younger brother, Shane, had also played the cello. According to everyone in the family, he'd been really, really good at it. He'd had a bright future as a musician—

But then something horrible had happened.

Marcus didn't know the details of Shane's death. Nobody talked about that part of the story.

All he knew was that Shane had been twelve years old when he died.

The same age as Marcus was now.

Maybe it was because of the age thing. Or maybe it was because Marcus was getting good at the cello. Whatever the case, it was freaking his mother out—and she was taking it out on him.

Which wasn't fair.

It wasn't like Marcus could stop playing. If he did, he'd be overwhelmed by all the music that no one else seemed to hear.

To Marcus, the sounds of the strings and the brass and the reeds were so bright and vibrant, the rhythms so wild and wicked, he couldn't believe that he was alone in his experience of it. And as a young child, he'd spoken incessantly about it, humming the melodies aloud so people would believe him.

Eventually his parents took him to see a doctor who suggested medication to stop the "hallucinations." Afterward, Marcus realized that maybe the music should become a secret instead. He didn't want it to end, even if it *was* all in his head.

This was around the time he'd finally begun to pick up whatever instrument was available from the music classroom at school and from his uncle's old collection at home to try to mimic the gorgeous melodies constantly floating around him.

It was a perfect transition: Stop talking about the music and start making it. This change alleviated his parents' fear, but it also invited attention from teachers and other adults who were fascinated by Marcus's sudden talent.

Though Marcus liked this attention, he wasn't sure he deserved it. Part of him felt like a fake; it wasn't as though he was inventing the compositions himself.

They were coming to him from somewhere beyond this world.

"Marcus."

He jerked the bow away from the strings and then opened his eyes. His mother was standing in the dining room doorway clutching a piece of paper. Marcus hadn't realized how lost he'd gotten in the music, nor how peaceful the afternoon had become. "Sorry, Mom," he said. "I was distracted."

To his surprise, she smiled. "It's okay." She held out the piece of paper to him. "I just got this message. Figured it was easier to print it out and bring it down to you."

"What is it?"

"Read it and find out."

Dear Mrs. Geller,

My name is L. Delphinium, and I am the director of the Larkspur Academy for the Performing Arts in New York State. I work with several professional scouts around the world, and when one of them attended your son's recent recital at the Oberlin campus in Ohio, she was overcome by the power of his performance. We would love it if Marcus came to study with us.

At Larkspur, Marcus will have access to the most accomplished visiting faculty from New York City's best companies. We have attached a file that includes our brochure with additional information about our music program and what we stand for.

We realize it is a little late in the season for an invitation such as this; however, it is our guiding principle that we seek out the most promising young talent, and we would be remiss if we did not at least try. With a student like Marcus, we would be willing to cover all tuition, board, and any travel expenses. It would cost you nothing.

Please let us know at your earliest convenience.

Best regards,
L. Delphinium
Director, Larkspur Academy

"Is this a joke?" Marcus asked.

"I can't imagine so."

"It's insane! There was a scout at the Oberlin recital?"

"You're a talented kid, Marcus," she said. "Don't act so surprised."

"And you wouldn't mind if I went?"

"I'd be *delighted* if you went." She folded her arms and grinned. She looked a little *too* delighted.

Before he could answer, a blast of noise resounded in Marcus's ears, a cacophony filled with instruments, too many to name. This wasn't like any music he'd ever heard before—it was more like a scream. Marcus flinched, and then, glancing at his mother, tried to disguise his shock as wide-eyed excitement.

She didn't hear it at all.

CHAPTER 3

IN THE DREAM that haunted her, Azumi Endo walked barefoot through the forest behind her aunt's home in Yamanashi Prefecture. The volcanic rock that had long ago spewed from the top of Mount Fuji made the ground there uneven and tricky beneath twisted tree roots and thick underbrush. Ignoring the clearly marked paths that crisscrossed the wilderness, Azumi often tripped, dropping to her knees, dirtying her nightgown before rising and continuing on. She knew that if she stopped even for a moment she might feel a hand on her shoulder, and if she turned around . . . well, she didn't want to imagine what she'd find looming behind her.

Tonight, she'd pushed farther than she ever had before, to a ravine where a drop-off sliced through the terrain. In the shadows and fog, she couldn't make out the bottom. One step forward and she would dive into a pit of sharp branches—a deadly trap rigged to ensnare her. She'd been following one of the long ribbons that had been tied to a trunk near the park's entrance, leading into the heart of the woods.

That was where the bodies were hidden.

In the dream, her skin was covered in a cool sheen of sweat, and her mind whirled, making her second-guess what direction to take. She couldn't lower herself down. The drop was too dangerous. Besides, it didn't seem likely that Moriko was there. Wouldn't she have answered Azumi's call? Azumi suddenly couldn't remember if she'd even been shouting out to Moriko, but she knew that she must have been. Wasn't that why she was there?

She was going to find her sister. She had to.

Now . . .

It was during moments like this—when Azumi began to question how she came to be alone in the middle of the forest at all—that she understood she was dreaming again. The shadow world of these woods was all in her mind. Or at least most of it was. There was another part of the dreaming, another part she never remembered until it was too late.

Because whenever Azumi dreamed of the forest, she also walked in her sleep.

Azumi opened her eyes to find herself surrounded by darkness, standing in the middle of the woods behind her family's house outside of Seattle for the third time that month.

An ocean now separated her from the haunted forest in Japan, but her mind insisted on closing that distance, putting her right back in the place where she'd lost her sister.

The mossy ground of Washington State was cold and wet against the soles of her feet, the summer air cool and humid. She could barely see in the darkness, uncertain whether the ravine had only been part of her dream, or if she was really a few steps from disaster.

Not now, not again, she thought, crouching down to protect herself against the night. *Mother and Father will be terrified*. How could she put them through this after what had happened to Moriko, after what Azumi herself had done?

She had lost her sister.

She couldn't lose herself.

The morning after Azumi's latest nightmare, an idea came to her about how she could protect both her parents and herself. She had to accept that if she were to stay home, her dreaming would bring her deeper into danger, closer to a place from which she too would not return.

On her computer, she searched for boarding schools on the East Coast of the US, as far from the Pacific Ocean as she could get.

Strangely, only a single website popped up.

The Larkspur School.

She tried the search again. And then again. She turned the computer off and then on—but the result was always the same.

Larkspur.

It must be some sort of sign, Azumi thought. *Maybe this is supposed to be* the one.

She glanced over the school's mission statement. *The Larkspur School has stood for over a century as a symbol of academic, artistic, and social excellence. Our pastoral campus is ideal for scholars who wish to shine . . .*

Azumi didn't need to read any more. This place sounded perfect.

CHAPTER 4

ONE OF THE producers barged into the sunny room where Dash and Dylan Wright had been waiting for the day to begin. "We're going to need you downstairs in fifteen," said the bouncy brunette, whose name neither boy could remember. "Just a heads up. 'Kay?"

They'd been trying to stem the boredom of their final production schedule by flipping through different game apps on their phones.

The Wright twins had been professional actors since the age of five, so they were used to all sorts of people coming and going into their lives, and dressing rooms, on a daily basis.

"Downstairs?" asked Dylan with a smirk. "For what? Are we shooting the next scene?" The producer raised an eyebrow and continued to look at Dash, as if only his reply mattered. Dylan waved at her, trying to get her attention. "Uh, hello? Am I invisible or something?"

"We're looking forward to it," said Dash apologetically. "Thanks." The producer blinked and then stomped off as if she couldn't wait to be far away from them both. Dash turned toward his brother with a glare. *Am I invisible or something?* he echoed, daggers in his eyes.

Dylan frowned. "What was I supposed to say? She completely ignored me."

Dash sighed and then shrugged. "I guess everyone's tired of your tricks."

"They're not tricks," said Dylan. "They're jokes!"

"Jokes don't usually end with people losing money. When you steal from people, they tend to dislike you."

"I made less money off them than you'd think." Dylan crossed him arms and set his jaw. "But who cares? After today, they won't have to put up with me any longer. I'm so ready to get out of this place."

The twins were nearly indistinguishable from each other. Both had the same dark skin, the same crooked, dimpled grin, the same bright black eyes, the same short curly hair.

They had been on the popular sitcom *Dad's So Clueless* since the age of five. The show was about a large family whose father was a hapless private investigator. For seven years, they'd shared the character of the youngest brother, a cutie-pie with a lisp whose name was Scooter but who was often called *Scoots Ba-Dooter*—a sickeningly sweet running gag that the twins eventually grew to despise, especially when people called them the name in real life.

Recently, the sitcom's head writer had decided to write Scoots off the show, sending the character to a boarding school in France. Today was the boys' last day of filming.

When they'd first received the news, Dash and Dylan were crushed. Dash had been particularly inconsolable, so much so that his parents had threatened to bring him to the emergency room unless he calmed himself down. He didn't tell anyone that he felt guilty for not trying harder to stop Dylan from playing his tricks . . . his "jokes." Maybe there was something he could have done that would have allowed them to continue working.

Dylan assured him that something better would come along. But the assurance didn't help.

Dash had recently begun to experience moments of extreme anxiety. For the past few weeks, he'd been having vivid nightmares about Dylan. In the nightmares, Dylan was in some sort of danger, and it was Dash's responsibility to save him. Dash would wake in the dark, racing down the hallway between their bedrooms to make sure Dylan was all right. Usually, he'd discover Dylan lying in his own bed, snoring softly, completely oblivious to his brother's worry.

Then, two nights ago, Dash had discovered his brother's bed empty—the sheets pulled back in a rumpled mess. Dash ran outside, into the night, turning down unfamiliar alleys and deserted back roads, until he found himself at a fenced-in, abandoned construction site about three miles from home. There, Dash had scrambled around the wide, pockmarked lot, screaming for his brother, expecting to find his broken body beneath a pile of rubble or trapped inside a Dumpster. But when his father showed up with the police they insisted that Dylan was at home, safe and sound.

Later, when Dash discovered Dylan lying in bed, his heart turned over with relief. He couldn't believe it. He'd been certain that Dylan had been out there, needing rescue.

Afterward, the boys had sat up in Dylan's room late into the night as Dash explained what he'd experienced. Dylan had teased Dash, telling him he needed to pull it together, or their parents were going to send him away to a boarding school in France, never to be seen again.

Dash had felt better, ready to fall back asleep, and Dylan offered to let him stay in his room. When Dylan had gotten up to turn off the light, Dash had caught a glimpse of his brother's bare feet.

Seconds later, in the new darkness, Dash had been too scared to say he'd seen a flash of Dylan in a strange bed, his soles black and bloody.

"Hey," said Dylan from the corner of the sunny room. "Did you read the email we just got?"

Dash shook his head. He'd been lost inside a game on his phone ever since the brown-haired woman had come to call them for the production meeting.

"Well, pull it up! This sounds like it might be really cool."

Dash saw a text from an unknown number as he unlocked his phone and swiped to the email app. The email's sender was Larkspur Productions, LLC. The subject read: *URGENT—NEW PROJECT FOR YOU.* Dash felt his stomach jolt.

Dylan! Dash!

What's up? Hope you boys are doing well. We're so glad to hear that the troubles with *Dad's So Clueless* haven't squashed your ambitions. As huge fans of Scooter, we knew we had to reach out to you regarding the amazing project we're putting together. We have a script that we'd love you to check out, ASAP.

We've read that you're both fans of horror films. Have we got something scary for you: a haunted house, several psychotic villains, and a plot filled with twists you'll never imagine! We believe that you two will be perfect for the lead roles: twin brothers who are the heroes of the story.

If you'd like to hear more, please let us know and we'll shoot the script right on over to you.

All the best,

Del Larkspur

President, Larkspur Productions, LLC

"Weird," Dylan said. "Right?"

Dash flinched. He hadn't noticed his brother had scrambled across the room to kneel on the floor by his chair. "Weird how?"

"Well, I mean, we'd both have to be our own person this time. We've only ever shared a role before."

"Did you think we'd be doing that for the rest of our lives?"

"No, but . . . you know, the producers always sort of thought your version of Scooter was better than mine."

"That's not even close to being true." Dash tried to keep his expression even. He knew his brother was right. He also believed it was one of the reasons Dylan had so often lashed out at the production crew. "On *this* show, we act exactly the same. Always."

Dylan rolled his eyes. "So . . . you'd consider saying yes?"

Dash was quiet for a moment, thinking about his terrible dreams. "I'm not sure about being in a *horror* movie."

Just then, both of their phones dinged. Another email had come through. Once again, the sender was Larkspur Productions, LLC. Wide-eyed, the boys stared at each other before opening the message.

Dash read it aloud. "Don't worry. The script isn't *too* scary." He glanced up at his brother, and then looked around the room, as if a hidden camera were pointed at them. He scoffed, then said, "Are they listening to us?"

"Oh yeah, totally," Dylan answered. "They're just *so* determined to get us there. Come on, Dash. The guy probably just had an afterthought. Stop being such a wuss."

"*You're* a wuss!" After a moment, Dash grinned. "It does feel good to be wanted again."

Dylan slapped his brother's knee. "We're going to be movie stars!"

"Okay then, who should write back?" asked Dash. "You or me?"

CHAPTER 5

POPPY HAD BEEN hiking up the hill from the Greencliffe train station for nearly fifteen minutes when she realized that someone was following her. Though leafy branches swayed and creaked high over her head and endless birdsong chimed from every direction, Poppy heard the sound of footsteps crunching gravel in the distance. She stopped and turned around. Behind her was a clear view of the path she'd walked minutes earlier— the curving country road, the towering greenery, and way in the distance, the glistening waters that transformed the Hudson River into a wide, jewel-encrusted ribbon.

When Poppy noticed the silhouette of a person at the bottom of the hill, she froze. She couldn't discern too many details, except that he looked small, maybe even smaller than she was.

He was dressed in a black jacket and khaki pants, and he was carrying a large object on his back—Poppy couldn't make it out.

Though the late August air was warm and the sun shone brightly, she felt a chill come upon her. She hitched her ratty pink messenger bag higher on her shoulder and continued walking up the hill, faster now, even though she wasn't sure she was even heading in the right direction.

In her bag, she carried her few possessions: a toothbrush, a face towel, a few pairs of socks and underwear, and her hollowed-out paperback copy of *The Lion, the Witch and the Wardrobe*, which was filled with several small trinkets that the Girl had left under her pillow. As heartbreaking as it had been, she'd had to leave her collection of books behind at Thursday's Hope. In the letter, Great-Aunt Delphinia had promised that once Poppy made it to Larkspur, she'd have everything in the world she'd ever want or need. New home, new school, new family. Before Poppy had managed to scrounge up the train fare to make the journey to Greencliffe, she wondered if this would include some friends too.

On the morning after she'd found the envelope in the filing cabinet, as Poppy brushed the tangles from her hair, the Girl finally appeared in the bathroom mirror again. But she no longer looked like the Girl who Poppy had grown up with. Her face was a strange blur, as if she were rapidly, unconsciously shaking her skull in all directions. Poppy felt as if she could hear the Girl screaming, after all this time finally trying to speak.

It was a message, Poppy understood. But what did it mean?

Before she'd had a chance to think, the mirror had turned black, as if the room on the other side—the reflected one in which the Girl was standing—had filled with thick, churning smoke. Poppy gasped.

A moment later, the mirror had cleared.

The Girl was gone again, taking the darkness with her.

Whenever the Girl had appeared since then, her face remained obscured by that disturbing and violent shaking.

It was such a disconcerting sight that Poppy began to avoid mirrors altogether.

When she heard footsteps coming up quickly on the road behind her, Poppy's instinct told her to run. But as soon as she took the first step, she stumbled on her shoelace and began to fall. She rolled onto the asphalt, twisting into a tumble, and then spun around to face the person who'd been chasing her, hands raised in protection.

To her surprise, no one was there. The trees swayed above her, light from the sky winking from between wide, green leaves.

Far away, around a bend in the road, she thought she could make out the sound of her fellow walker dragging his heels.

So who had she just heard? Had the person dashed away into the woods? Maybe he was watching from somewhere off the road, between the trees.

Crazy Poppy, she heard in her head—the voices of the girls from Thursday's Hope taunting her still. *Crazy Poppy. Craaaazy Poppyyyy.*

To gain her bearings, she stood and took in her surroundings. In the dense brush a few feet away, a tall stone wall was camouflaged by twisted red vines and thin saplings, running alongside the road's shoulder. Was this the boundary of Great-Aunt Delphinia's estate?

A dozen yards ahead, Poppy saw a wide gravel path branching off the main road into the woods. Where the path intersected the wall, a space in the stonework opened up like a missing tooth in a wide, dead grin. Two pillars climbed up from the forest floor to form an entryway. An ornamental iron railing connected the two pillars, its rusted curlicues broken and twisted as if someone with abnormal strength had wrenched it apart. Below, where one would expect to find a pair of decorative gates, the space was empty, the woods beyond forming a tunnel that darkened as it went deeper.

The sight made her mouth dry. Poppy stepped forward, then stopped at the edge of the driveway. That was when she noticed words engraved on stones in the center of each pillar: *Larkspur*.

This *was* the place. Her new home.

With tall grass and weeds growing in sporadic patches at her feet, the driveway looked like it hadn't been crossed in decades. Confusion rattled her brain.

Crazy Poppy . . .

Poppy squeezed her eyes shut. *Stop it!*

Maybe there was another gate farther up the road—one that Great-Aunt Delphinia used more frequently.

These thoughts flew away when Poppy noticed something else carved into the pillars, directly beneath the name of the estate—a familiar symbol, a picture that Poppy could have drawn from memory. The outline of a bird. The image was the same as the twisted wire sculpture that the Girl had removed from the pocket of her pinafore all those years ago, the first present that Poppy had found under her pillow the next morning.

Something crunched the gravel directly behind her.

Wide-eyed, Poppy stiffened. She glanced over her shoulder to find the road deserted. Footsteps moved all around her. "Hello?" she whispered. There was no one there. No one that Poppy could see.

Poppy knew of another way, one that she was terrified to try. But she had to find out . . .

Trembling, she removed her clamshell compact from her satchel and flipped it open. As she brought up the mirror to eye level, she was certain of who would be there.

But this time when she peered into the glass, she jolted.

In the mirror, the Girl was standing several steps behind her. Now, however, the Girl's whole body was shaking. She jerked with lightning-quick spasms, flickering like an image in a sped-up film.

Before Poppy could respond, the Girl bolted forward.

Coldness encircled her as the Girl's arms twisted around Poppy's torso and squeezed. Poppy felt herself yanked backward into the road, away from Larkspur's gate. As she collapsed to the ground, she released a scream of such terror it sent all the songbirds careening nervously from the safety of the high branches, screeching like echoes of her own voice up into the air. They dissipated as Poppy lost her breath, and the sky beyond turned dark.

CHAPTER 6

A SHRIEK RANG out from around the bend in the road ahead, and Marcus Geller nearly dropped his cello. Seconds later, the sound came to an abrupt end, and he grew even more nervous. Could the cry have come from the girl he'd seen leaving the train station before him? Was she hurt?

Marcus laid his things on the side of the road, and took off in a sprint.

As he rounded the bend, Marcus saw the girl from the train station lying in the middle of the road, not moving. "Hey!" he yelled as he ran the last couple of dozen yards. "Are you okay?" Kneeling beside her, he realized that he had no idea what to do. She was on her back, her arms splayed out, her knees bent, her head turned away from him. "Please be alive," he whispered, holding his hand in front of her nose. Warm breath tickled his skin, and he released a sigh.

He knew he had to get her out of the road—at any moment, a car could come speeding around the corner. He took her hand, figuring it might at least get her attention.

The girl's eyelids fluttered and then opened. When she saw him leaning over her, a look of confusion quickly transformed into terror. Eyes like mirrors, she opened her mouth and screamed again, and she and Marcus scrambled away from each other, crouching in the road as if about to spar.

After a moment, Marcus remembered that he'd been the one who'd approached her. He took a slow breath and then held out his hands to show her he meant no harm. "It's okay," he said. "I was trying to help."

As he rose to his feet, the girl reached for the pink bag that was lying on the nearby shoulder of the road and pulled it close to her, as if he might try to steal it. Then she did the same thing to a small black makeup compact, clutching it in one fist.

A second later, she whipped her arm back and then threw the compact across the road as hard as she could.

It skipped like a stone upon water before disappearing into the dense scrub. With a sigh of relief, she wiped her nose with the back of her wrist, glanced up at Marcus, and shook her head.

Marcus felt like he'd just met a girl who'd been raised by wolves.

"I'm Marcus," he said purposefully, as if she might not understand him. "I was down the street when I heard you scream. You were just lying here." The girl blinked and then glanced around. She looked like she expected to see someone else there with them, maybe hiding in the brush. "I'm sorry," he went on when he realized she didn't plan on answering him. "I didn't mean to scare you."

"You're not the one who scared me," said the girl, continuing to examine the trees.

Marcus's skin tingled. His mother had told him he might meet different sorts of people at Larkspur, but this girl was just plain weird. Then again, many musical prodigies were, so he knew he shouldn't be surprised. He wanted to ask her, *If I'm not the one who scared you, then who is?* Instead he said, "Let's get out of the road. Maybe you can tell me what happened."

She finally met his gaze and gave him a look that said she had *no idea* what had happened. But she stood and brushed herself off, and headed toward a stony path that veered from the pavement and edged into the woods. Marcus noticed the wall and the gate standing several yards back, as well as the word *Larkspur*, which was engraved in each stone pillar.

"Oh," he said, startled. "We're here. We've made it."

The girl scowled at him. "What do you mean?" she asked.

"To Larkspur," he said, blushing. "I'm sorry—isn't this where you were headed too?"

"Yes," she responded unsurely.

Marcus spent a moment observing the decay of the entry and the dark tunnel of trees beyond the wall. A soft and melancholy piano melody drifted to him on the wind from somewhere close by. It was the same tune he'd heard the musician behind the wall playing on the day he'd gotten his invitation to Larkspur. The girl didn't notice the music. But then, he didn't imagine that she would. No one ever did. "This isn't really what I expected," he said. "What about you?"

"What do you mean?"

"Is it what you expected?"

The girl looked confused. "I-I don't know," she stammered. "What's your name again?"

"Marcus Geller," he said slowly. She must have hit her head when she'd fallen. Hard.

"And why did you come to Larkspur House?"

"Well, I was invited. Weren't you?" She didn't answer. His nerves kept him talking. "I'm cello mostly, but I like to experiment with other instruments too. Piano. Flute. Harmonica! Harmonica is so much fun." He reached into his back pocket and pulled out the small steel instrument he'd stowed there before leaving Ohio. He held it to his lips and then performed a brief, jazzy riff. "What do you play?" he asked.

"Play?"

"Yeah, what instrument?"

"I don't play an instrument."

"A singer, then. Sweet! You look like you have a nice voice."

The girl's cheeks turned the same pink shade as her bag. "I do?" Her voice was suddenly very soft.

"Totally. I can tell these things. Listen, I dropped all my stuff when I heard . . . well, never mind. Would you mind waiting for me? When I get back, we can walk to the house together." *And then you can tell me what you were doing lying in the road.* "It's got to be just up that path, don't you think?" The girl glanced over her shoulder and into the woods. Then, with her lips pressed together, she turned back and nodded. "You going to be all right alone?" Marcus asked. She straightened her shoulders and tucked her hair behind her ears.

He interpreted that as a *yes.*

After he'd taken several steps down the road toward his bags, he heard a muffled voice come from behind him. Glancing back, he saw the girl watching him. She'd said something that he'd missed.

"Poppy," the girl repeated. "My name is Poppy Caldwell."

The piano melody echoed out again, but it had changed, becoming more upbeat—not quite happy, but certainly not as sad. He instantly thought of it as "Larkspur's Theme," a song that belonged to this place. When he and Poppy reached the house, he'd have to find a piano and play it so she could hear it too.

"Nice to meet you, Poppy Caldwell," Marcus said with a smile.

"And thanks," she managed. "For helping me get up."

He gave her a quick salute and surprised a laugh from her. Okay, so maybe she wasn't completely weird after all.

Marcus had never been away from home for more than a weekend, and here he was, by himself in upstate New York getting ready to spend the year on a full scholarship at the prestigious Larkspur Academy for the Performing Arts. He was about to eat, breathe, and live music with a whole bunch of other talented kids who thought just like him, with no interference from his mom or his brothers and sister. He couldn't believe it.

Maybe, Marcus thought as he came upon his bag and large black case on the side of the road, *there will be people at the academy who experience the world in the same way I do. Maybe I'll meet others who geek out about Chet Baker, Dave Brubeck, and Nina Simone as much as me.*

He found Poppy standing right where he'd left her: at the gravel path that led to the shadowy gap in the stone wall. She looked worried.

"Ready?" he asked. Poppy nodded. Together they stepped forward. "So," Marcus ventured, "do you want to tell me what happened?"

Poppy bit at her lip for a few seconds. Then she said, "Could you tell me more about your invitation to Larkspur?"

"I'm pretty sure it's the same one you got."

"That's the thing," she said as they crossed under the twisted iron railing and past the pillars into the shadowy tunnel of trees, "I'm pretty sure it's not."

CHAPTER 7

AFTER THE DRIVER her parents had hired left her at Larkspur's gate, Azumi dragged her luggage deep into the woods and up the slow ascent, memories of her dark dreams scratching icy branches along her spine.

The previous summer, Azumi and her sister, Moriko, had visited their auntie Wakame at her home just northwest of Mount Fuji on the island of Honshu. Auntie Wakame had forbidden the girls from entering the nearby forest on their own, since it was so common for even frequent visitors to become lost there. With its thick canopy of trees that hid the sun and the iron-filled volcanic rock that messed with compass needles, the national park was known as one of the most haunted spots in all of Japan.

Azumi had promised herself she'd never go back to Yamanashi Prefecture again. But the farther she strolled up

Larkspur's driveway, the distance between the present and the past became shorter and shorter. Everywhere she looked, she recognized parts of the forest where Moriko had disappeared— lichen-covered tree trunks, dappled shadows dancing on the leafy ground, dew clinging to low-hanging, delicate mosses.

Then, with a blink, she was there. Back in Japan. Remembering that horrible day.

"Come on, Azumi," said Moriko, stepping off the clearly marked path. "Don't be such a scaredy-cat."

"I'm *not* a scaredy-cat." Azumi looked around in disgust. "I just think that Auntie Wakame might have a point. Anyone could be hiding in there."

"You can hide too. And while you're hiding, *I* can look for more treasure."

"Treasure? You really think the garbage that the tourists leave behind is worth digging through?"

"Of course! How else do you think an explorer ever finds anything of value?"

"That's deep, Moriko, Treasure Hunter." Azumi scanned the nylon ribbons that crossed the demarcated trails and veered off into the forbidden parts of the woods, disappearing into the shadows. The ribbons came in all different colors, each of them bright so they could be easily spotted by a ranger or a visitor to the park. "Why are all these ribbons here?"

Moriko looked over at her. "People drive out from Tokyo. Sad people. They come here to . . . say good-bye to the world. They tie these ribbons at the edge of the forest so that someone can find them after they're gone. Some say it's *their* ghosts that haunt these woods."

"Like in Auntie's yūrei tales?"

Moriko made her eyes wide, her blue hair changing shades in the dimming light. "Exactly!"

Azumi shook her head, trying to look exhausted or annoyed—anything but the terror she felt bubbling in her gut. "No thanks. I'm not ruining my new sneakers. You go on. Have fun. You always do."

"Azumi!" Moriko called out. "I'm kidding! Don't be like that!"

But Azumi walked away. She hurried along the lonely trails back to their aunt's cottage as the sun began to set.

Her sister did not return to Auntie Wakame's that night.

Their parents traveled immediately from Washington. The search for Moriko was long and exhaustive. No one turned up a single shred of evidence. Not the Ministry of the Environment, not the local police and detectives, not the family.

And Azumi never saw her sister again.

The dreams started shortly after Azumi returned to the United States. It was as if the trees behind her own home had become spirits of the bodies that littered the Japanese forest, calling to her, the hush of a breeze meeting the branches outside her bedroom window like whispers in her head. *Here. Here we are. Come and get us, child. Come and help us find our way home.*

Larkspur's driveway made a sharp turn, and a giant meadow domed by a gleaming blue sky opened up before Azumi. All at once the forest and its shadows were gone.

Perched on the crest of the slope, nearly two hundred yards farther up the path, was the grand structure that she'd first seen online a month ago.

The Larkspur School.

It looked quite different in real life. So much bigger. She took in its steeply pitched roofline and many gabled windows, its ivy-encrusted stone porches, the glinting windows that shone like ice against the dark stone walls, the turrets that lifted up like dark mounds of whipped dessert from the ends of what looked like passageways, and the soaring tower that appeared to spike straight through its massive granite heart.

When Azumi reached the center of the porch, she knocked on the French doors, but no one answered. She opened one of the doors and peered at the shadows just inside. She heard nothing—no footsteps, no talking, not even the tick of a clock.

"Hello?" she called out. "I'm Azumi Endo, and I'm here for school!" But no one answered. "Excuse me! Is anyone here?!"

Azumi tossed her suitcase just inside the door and then sat on the wide stone porch she'd seen from the path. Someone would come by eventually. Until then, she'd take pictures on her phone to send to her parents.

Moriko and Azumi had always been opposites. Several years older than Azumi, Moriko had pierced her nose and dyed her hair and listened religiously to their parents' old punk-rock albums. Moriko's classmates had looked up to her as if she were a superstar, a trendsetter, a kind soul, and a creative spirit. The memorial in the high school yearbook had taken up two pages.

Azumi kept her own hair long and straight and black as night, as it was meant to be. Admiring a clean look, she didn't put up posters on her walls. She always took off her shoes at the front door, just as her baaba had taught her. Azumi didn't have a clue what her own memorial might look like if her friends were to make one, but she would have liked it to contain her seventh grade yearbook photo, the serious one in which she looked like a lawyer or a judge, her mouth downturned slightly and her eyebrow raised in a way that said, *Don't even think about it.*

When Azumi turned thirteen, she realized that she could never be as carefree as Moriko had been. But she could become a diligent daughter and please her parents in all the ways Moriko had refused to: with awesome grades, and the most goals during soccer matches, and *classy* friends who were as determined to succeed as she was. This was why her sleepwalking had been such a nightmare over the past year. She was losing control. Just like she'd lost Moriko. It made her want to scream.

On her phone's screen, Azumi noticed a figure moving near the line of trees, several hundred feet from where she'd exited the woods. Lowering the phone, however, she discovered nothing there but the breeze moving the dense, leafy growth, which caught the sun occasionally, making it *seem* as though someone had been watching her.

She lifted the phone's camera back up to take the picture anyway. When a black patch appeared in the same spot on the screen, Azumi inhaled a sharp little breath and looked closer. The patch wavered before the tree line, as if an impenetrable shadow were being cast on that spot from about six or seven feet above the ground.

A human-shaped shadow.

She took a picture, then zoomed in.

Long, thin arms, sticklike legs, and a head that appeared way too large to be carried on such a gaunt frame.

And eyes. Two sparks of gold, watching her.

The image shuddered, and the screen went black.

In her peripheral vision, Azumi noticed movement by the tree line. She stood, ready to bolt away. But then two kids emerged from the mouth of the woods. A boy and a girl. They were carrying luggage.

Raising her hand over her head, Azumi waved emphatically to the two travelers. They paused on the path and waved back slowly. She had just lowered her hand, not wanting to look overeager, when she noticed that, off the path to their left, standing in the meadow where she'd first noticed its presence, the dark shadow had reappeared.

Slowly, it turned its head toward the boy and girl.

Watching them.

About to pounce.

As Azumi opened her mouth to shout out a warning, the shadow lunged.

"Hey!" she cried. "Over here!"

Don't be such a scaredy-cat.

. . . Shut up, Moriko!

The boy and the girl stopped on the path, staring at her in confusion. Azumi waved them forward, swinging both arms up and back over her head. The dark thing was closing in on them, and they had no idea.

"Hurry!" *Closer. Closer.* "Run!"

Something seemed to click for the pair, and they took off across the grass, sprinting toward the porch. The shadow creature loomed large, gaining ground.

"Don't turn around!"

They weren't going to make it.

Azumi dashed down the porch steps.

In the meadow, the shadow's golden eyes seemed to flicker with delight that Azumi was approaching.

She concentrated on the boy and the girl, who were now only a couple of dozen feet away. "Toss your bag to me!" she shouted to the boy as he came up beside her. She grunted as she caught his luggage, but she managed to hold it tight. He wore another case strapped to his shoulders, something that looked like an enormous backpack.

Azumi turned toward the house.

A rushing, sucking sound came quickly behind them as they raced up the steps to the porch. Azumi didn't look back, not even when she swung open the glass door and pushed the others into the dark entry. Slamming the door shut behind them, she scrambled to find a lock or a latch to hold it closed.

She expected the shadow to barrel into the door at any moment.

But instead . . . nothing.

Through the window, she could see that the meadow and the porch were as empty as they'd been when she'd first arrived. No shadow. No flickering golden eyes. She tried to swallow a deep breath but released an embarrassing squeak instead.

"What's going on?" asked the boy.

Azumi turned, breathless. "I-I'm sorry. I was certain I saw . . ." She glanced over her shoulder again just to be sure. She felt her shoulders tense. "Something was chasing you."

"An animal?" asked the girl, staring wide-eyed out at the morning.

"Well, yeah, it was an animal. A *big* animal. It looked . . . angry." Azumi shook her head. "I can't believe you didn't see it. It was literally about to bite your heads off."

The boy stood by the window, wearing a slight grin, as if he didn't believe her. "It must be hiding now."

"*Obviously*," said Azumi. "I mean, it didn't just disappear!"

"I guess we should thank you," said the girl. "For saving us?"

"If you're going to laugh at me, then next time, you can just *save yourselves*." The boy and the girl looked like she'd just slapped them. Azumi shook her head, embarrassed that she'd allowed herself to say such a thing. "Anyway, my name is Azumi. Azumi Endo."

"I'm Poppy. And this is—"

"Marcus." The boy brushed his red curls away from his forehead and then saluted. He adjusted the straps of the thing he carried on his back, and Azumi realized from the shape of it that it must be a cello.

"Do you know where we can find the others?" asked Azumi.

"The others?" Marcus echoed.

"The other students. The faculty. Anyone." Azumi watched as Marcus glanced at Poppy, as if they knew something that she did not. "What is it? Did I say something funny again?"

"I don't have a clue where anyone is," he said, ignoring her question, the odd expression dropping from his face. "But it's probably a good idea if we take a look around. Right, Poppy?"

Poppy stood there, hugging her rib cage. "I guess so."

"Okay then," said Azumi, picking up her bag. "Good." She peered once more through the windows out at the sunny meadow. Even though she couldn't see it anymore, she was sure the shadow was still out there somewhere—hiding, watching, waiting.

CHAPTER 8

DASH AND DYLAN had insisted that the driver of their limo pull all the way onto the Larkspur property, claiming that they'd pay for any damage that the creeping foliage inflicted on the car.

As the car drove off and left them alone, the boys found a pair of wide wooden doors. They knocked and knocked, but no one answered. Pressing their ears to the glass, the boys listened for a response. Inside, they could hear the echoes of their pounding.

They texted Del to see where he was. But the messages failed to send. *No service.*

"What are we going to do now?" asked Dash. Dylan answered by stepping forward and pressing the latch on the door handle. The doors swung inward with a resounding groan. "Oh yeah." Dash forced a chuckle. "I didn't think of that."

"Good thing I'm here, little brother."

"You know I hate it when you call me that. Being born five minutes after you doesn't make me 'littler' than you."

"You're so right," said Dylan. "*I know* you hate it." He smiled that smile that always made Dash nervous, the one that Dash could never pull off, not even when he practiced in a mirror. The smile that said, *Don't be a wuss*. They weren't perfectly identical after all, Dash knew, especially when it came to their personalities.

With his stomach churning, Dash followed Dylan into the mansion. Inside, his gaze flitted around the cathedral-size room. He took in the details—the wide oak banisters that bordered the central stairway, the wood pillars that rose to the pointed, arched ceiling, the high stained-glass windows that allowed shocking streaks of red and blue and gold light to filter across the intricate, circular parquet floor.

The boys placed their bags in its center.

A harsh tone bounced around the room, ringing in Dash's ears, making him feel dizzy and disoriented. He blinked and saw Dylan standing a few feet away, struggling with his phone.

"Stupid thing," Dylan said.

"What's wrong?"

"Someone keeps calling me, but every time I pick up, the phone goes dead."

"What's the number?"

"It says *unknown*."

"Service here bites."

"But what if Del is trying to get in touch with us? To tell us where to go?"

"Why don't we try to find him?"

Dylan smiled. "Do you want to head upstairs or should I?"

"We should stick together, don't you think?" Dash asked, trying to sound unafraid.

He peered at the grand staircase and froze.

A boy was standing at the bottom, staring at them. He was dressed in dark shorts and a white button-down shirt. But that wasn't what caught Dash's attention. The boy was wearing a mask. A white rabbit with shadowy cutout eyes and a big, pink grin for a mouth.

Dash had a bad feeling—it made him want to turn around and walk away.

When Dylan saw the boy, he called out, "Hey, yo! What's up?"

The boy in the rabbit mask didn't answer. He only continued to stare. "We're looking for Del," Dash added. "Any clue where we can find him?"

The boy in the mask took off, disappearing up the worn marble stairs.

"Hey!" Dylan shouted, hurrying after him. "Wait!"

Dash followed closely, not wanting to be left alone. But when they'd made it halfway to the first landing, Dylan jerked to a stop as if someone had yanked on his spine. Dash reached up to catch his brother before he toppled, but Dylan crashed into him, knocking him off-balance.

Limbs tangled together, they tumbled down the steps all the way to the bottom.

Something like a memory flashed through Dylan's mind. He flinched, cringing at the white-hot blast that burned inside his skull. His entire body prickled with electricity.

The world around him disappeared. He was back in the dressing room on the set of *Dad's So Clueless*. Dash was racing toward him from out of a mass of shadows, his arms outstretched, his face contorted, screaming in anger or pain. A booming sound rattled his eardrums, followed quickly by something that sounded a bit more human—a mewling, crying whisper.

The back of Dylan's skull felt like it had exploded. Little glittering lights swam around what was left of his blurred vision. Then, as the brunt of the sensation began to fade, Dylan understood that the whine was coming from his own throat.

"Dylan? Dylan, are you all right?"

Dylan realized he was lying down, the wooden floor of the foyer cold beneath him. Dash's face hovered over him, eyes wide, looking paralyzed with worry. For some reason, this annoyed Dylan. "Why are you looking at me like that?"

Glancing over his brother's shoulder, he noticed the staircase rising steeply. "I must have tripped."

"You *didn't* trip, Dylan. Something happened to you. It was like a seizure. You knocked us both down the stairs."

"Don't be ridiculous. I don't have seizures."

Dash leaned away, sitting back on his heels. "Fine. Whatever. You're perfectly healthy." He sighed, frustrated. "But you hit your head pretty hard on the way down. It echoed."

Dylan sat up, rubbing the back of his skull. His heart was beating too fast, and he worried that whatever had just happened might happen again. But he couldn't let his brother know. For the past few weeks, Dash had been super worried about him. "Well, I'm okay now." This had happened at least twice before, each time accompanied by a horrifying vision of Dash running toward him, reaching out to either claw or catch him. "Jeez, Dash, sometimes you're worse than Mom and Dad."

"Do you think you can stand up? Maybe we should walk back to town and call for help."

"No way."

Dash rolled his eyes "But, Dylan, you're not—"

"If we find that kid, the one in the mask, maybe he'll help us."

Dash shivered. "I didn't get that sense from him, Dylan. He was full-on creepy."

Footsteps echoed through the cavernous chamber. Dylan turned to see who it was.

Emerging from the shadows was a girl with long black hair that draped far below her shoulder blades. She was dressed in a fitted denim jacket and a long black dress. Another girl with messy dirty-blond hair walked beside the first, wearing a faded purple T-shirt and jeans, clutching a bright-pink messenger bag. Behind them was a boy, who appeared to be carrying a tall backpack of some sort. He wore a black sports jacket and khaki pants. His dark red hair lifted from his scalp in wide curls.

Is this the rest of the film's cast?

Dylan struggled to his feet. He stepped forward, holding out his hand. If he was going to succeed on this set, he knew he had to make the best impression before his brother could beat him to it.

"Hey," he said, laying on the California cool-kid charm that his agents had drilled into him long ago. "How's it going? Dylan Wright." He glanced over at Dash, who looked at him in surprise. "And this is my brother—"

"Dylan, sit down!" Dash commanded harshly. "You might have a concussion!"

A flash of anger jolted down Dylan's spine and rippled in the pit of his stomach. Keeping his face even, he chuckled nervously as the group stared at the twins. "I'm sorry," he said. "My brother can be a little dramatic. Have any of you seen Del?"

CHAPTER 9

POPPY COULDN'T BELIEVE her eyes. Standing before her was one of her favorite television characters: Scooter Underwood from *Dad's So Clueless*. And seated beside him was another version. Two Scoots Ba-Dooters were staring at her as if she might present them with a key to the house.

This must be in my head, she thought. Blood pounded in her ears, and she heard the girls from Thursday's Hope chanting again. *Crazy. Poppy. Crazy. Poppy.*

But now Marcus was making introductions. "Hi, I'm Marcus. This is Poppy and Azumi." Azumi waved as Poppy remained frozen, unsure of herself. "Are you students here too?"

The seated boy finally stood and brushed himself off. "I'm Dash. Dylan's brother. And, um, no, we're not *students here*."

Marcus frowned and shook his head slightly.

"You guys are actors," said Azumi. "I've seen you on television."

Actors, thought Poppy. Not the real Scoots, but the boys who played him. Twins.

"Yeah," said Dylan. "Aren't you guys actors too?"

"No," said Marcus cautiously. "I'm here on a music scholarship. Azumi's here for academics. And Poppy . . . Well, Poppy's story is kind of complicated."

Poppy couldn't keep herself from blushing. *Complicated* was an understatement. She hunched her shoulders, though she knew she was only making herself look more foolish, like an ostrich hiding its head in the sand.

"Dylan," said Dash, placing his hand on his brother's shoulder, "I really wish you'd sit down." He turned to the trio. "He just fell down the stairs."

"Do you always let your brother talk to you like he's your dad?" Azumi asked Dylan, hands on her hips.

Dash flinched. "I was only trying to—"

"We *both* fell down the stairs," Dylan growled before looking at the group again with a forced smile. "But we're both perfect now. Promise. So . . . if you're not in the cast, you must be on the crew."

63

"The crew?" asked Azumi.

"Why are you here?" A hint of frustration slipped into Dylan's otherwise smooth voice.

"Marcus already told you," said Azumi. "This is our school."

"Why are *you* here?" Marcus retorted.

Dash spoke up. "Del Larkspur is filming a new horror movie. We're playing the leads."

"Del Larkspur?" Poppy squeaked. "Did you say *Del Larkspur*?"

Dylan sighed. "Finally, we're getting somewhere. You know Del?"

Poppy's voice was so soft Dylan had to strain to hear it. "Well . . . no. My great-aunt invited me to live with her. But her name is *Delphinia* Larkspur."

"Could they be the same person?" asked Dash. "We thought Del was a guy, but maybe Del is actually Delphinia."

Poppy's spine tingled and her fingers felt numb. None of this seemed right. "In her letter, my great-aunt didn't say anything about making a movie." She thought back to watching *Dad's So Clueless* in the common room at Thursday's Hope with the other girls, remembering the warm feeling it gave her to see a funny family portrayed on the small screen. To see parents get mad at their nutty kids but then forgive them at the end of every episode because they just loved them so much.

"Hold up," said Dylan, shaking his head, squinting. "What letter?"

Azumi exhaled sharply as she shuffled through her shoulder bag and removed the printout she'd already showed Poppy and Marcus. Marcus followed suit, taking out the email his mother had received from the music school. They handed the pages to the twins. Poppy scrambled to show them her own handwritten letter. The boys scanned everything quickly, and then Dylan pulled his phone from his pocket, opening the message from Larkspur Productions, LLC. After a few seconds, the group looked up at one another, and then glanced around the chamber as if someone were watching them.

"This is weird," said Dash. "Look at the names: *L. Delphinium* wrote to Marcus's mom. *Del Larkspur* and *Delphinia Larkspur* wrote to us and to . . ." He glanced at Poppy, self-conscious. "I'm sorry, what's your name again?"

"Poppy," she said, her voice cracking. She crossed her arms, feeling suddenly cold.

"Right." Dash handed back the invitations, emails, and brochures. "The details don't really add up. I mean, it feels like someone is messing with us."

"Not necessarily," said Marcus, looking around the room. "This house seems big enough for all of it. A school, a filming location, a home."

Azumi spoke up. "Still, it's strange. Earlier, Marcus found Poppy lying in the road in front of the main gate."

"What were you doing in the road?" asked Dylan.

Poppy's eyes went wide. "I'm not really sure. I guess I fainted or something." The twins were looking at her like she was a total freak. Her group-home defenses immediately kicked in. "Speaking of strange, Azumi saw some sort of creature out in the meadow by the woods. She thought it was chasing me and Marcus. But when we all reached the house, the meadow was empty."

"I never said it was a *creature*." Azumi's face lit up, red. "I said it was an animal. A big animal. And I have a picture." She dug in her pocket for her phone and swiped it open. But after a few seconds, she furrowed her eyebrows. "It was right here. A black smudge. It had golden, glowing eyes. It looked like . . . I don't know what." She handed her phone around. When Poppy got it, the image on the screen was of the sunny meadow, clear of any blotches or unusual shadows.

"*We* saw a boy at the top of the stairs," said Dash. "He was wearing a rabbit mask."

"Weird," said Marcus. "It would be really nice if we could find an *adult*."

"Like my great-aunt," said Poppy.

"Like a teacher," said Azumi.

"Like someone on the crew," said Dylan.

Dash stepped away from the group and peered up the staircase. "Hello?" he called out, the echo of his voice fluttering around the upper rafters like bats trapped inside the house. "Is anybody here?" The group waited in silence, but no one answered.

CHAPTER 10

AZUMI AND MARCUS placed their luggage in the center of the grand room, beside the twins' stuff. Poppy held on to her bag.

"The boy in the mask ran up the stairs," said Dylan. "Maybe we should go check up there."

Not listening, Azumi disappeared with Marcus through one of the doorways off the foyer. A moment later, she called out, "Whoa. You guys have to see this!"

Poppy paused in the doorway, looking back at the twins. "Coming?" she asked, her voice quavering and small. The boys reluctantly followed.

Marcus stood just inside the entry of a long room.

The space looked like it had been set up for an extravagant

party. Red and white paper streamers hung from high places, drooping down from the corners of bookshelves that were stocked with old board games and puzzles, running up toward the tall windows that lined one long wall, and continuing in daisy chains all the way to the entry. Loose balloons meandered across a thick Persian rug, pushed by what must have been a draft that Marcus couldn't feel. They looked like scurrying animals sniffing around for scraps of birthday cake. The couches and chairs arranged to face the center of the chamber were worn, as if they had been sitting there for a century, getting good use from the children who must have played here.

It's a music school, Marcus thought, eyeing the four other kids. *It has to be.* He drummed his fingers on his stomach and closed his eyes for a moment, itching to get his hands on an instrument. How strange would he look if he grabbed his cello and got down to it right here? The familiar tune continued to play in Marcus's head, the melody still as sweet as blueberry pie. But it was getting louder and louder, and Marcus had to bite at his lip to keep from shouting out to the Musician that he'd heard enough.

Someone squeezed his waist and shouted, "Boo!"

Marcus nearly screamed as Dylan jumped out from behind him.

Dylan burst out laughing, as Dash came up and punched his

arm. "Starting early?" Dash asked, his eyes slivered. He tossed an apologetic look at Marcus, but Marcus couldn't bring himself to smile. Everyone else was staring at him like he was some sort of nutjob. It made him think about how his brothers and sister had looked at him when they learned that the doctors had suggested medication to correct his "hallucinations."

"Dude, I'm sorry," said Dylan, wiping away the last of his laughter. "You looked so intense. Like you were arguing with yourself. I just had to do something about it. You okay?"

"I-I'm fine." Marcus nodded. "Thanks for your *concern* though."

The others strolled before the shelves, examining the trove of games. "Do you guys think the decorations are for us?" he asked. *It's a nice gesture*, Marcus thought. Though it would have been nicer if someone had been here to greet them . . . *and* if someone had answered him.

A strange-looking sphere made out of gray wire sat on a table in front of the windows. On one side of the contraption, there was a handle, bent like an S, as if it were meant to be turned like a crank. Inside the sphere were dozens of little red balls. Curious, Marcus made his way to the table. His grandmother had once taken him to bingo night in the basement of St. Luke's back in Ohio. The person calling the game had used a globe like this to call the numbers. Marcus touched the handle and then gave the sphere a spin. The balls inside rattled and one slid out into a small chute, hitting the table with a satisfying plink.

Marcus picked up the ball and turned it over. There was no number on it, only the letter *L* marked in white. *Weird*, he thought. *Bingo doesn't work like that*. He gave the sphere another turn. Out popped the letter *E*, then *T*. Marcus stopped cranking the handle, but little balls continued to roll out, each one stopping with the letter facing toward him. *L*, *E*, and *T* were followed by *S*, *P*, *L*.

LETSPL

Two more balls rolled free.

LETSPLAY

LETS PLAY.

Something cold shivered inside Marcus. "Um, guys?" he called, suddenly wishing he were fifteen feet closer to the rest of the group.

Azumi was standing on her toes, reaching for a large paper parcel that was high up on one of the shelves. "What's that?" Poppy asked. As Azumi grabbed for the sack, it tumbled off the shelf, and its contents spilled onto the floor. The girls yelped and leapt back.

Marcus only had a brief glimpse of what was in the bag. It looked like small human bodies.

CHAPTER 11

AZUMI DIDN'T KNOW why she had been so drawn to the large paper bag on the shelf above her, but now that the parcel was lying torn at her feet, she felt sick.

There were five dolls splayed on the floor in front of her. They were made out of stiff papier-mâché, nothing a child would play with. Their features, including the clothes, had been painted on with vibrant, glossy acrylics.

The two dolls on the far left were painted light brown and were dressed in shorts, graphic T-shirts, and sandals. Beside them lay a girl with pale skin and splotchy freckles. Dark gold paper hair lay across her shoulders, where a pink satchel had been painted directly onto her body. Next was a boy with red hair. The details of his curls were shaded expertly, giving the illusion that you could pull on a strand and it would spring back to the paper skull with a *boing!* He wore a black sports jacket, khaki pants, and a convincingly dirty pair of white Converse All Stars. Finally, on the far right, was a girl with long dark hair. Her denim jacket was painted to appear buttoned tight, and her black dress stopped just above thin ankles.

"It's us," said Marcus quietly.

"They're even wearing our clothes," said Poppy, reaching out toward the one that looked like her, stopping just before she touched it.

"How?" asked Dash.

"Someone painted them on," said Marcus.

"I can see that," said Dash. "But handmade stuff like this takes time. The prop people on our set out in Hollywood would've needed at least a day to prep for something like this. This paint is dry."

"How did whoever made these know what we'd be wearing today?" asked Poppy.

"Look . . ." Azumi reached forward and touched a piece of twine that was looped around the neck of her papier-mâché counterpart. The other figurines were the same. They were all wearing nooses. Azumi grasped the string attached to the one that looked like her and lifted the thing from the floor. The Azumi doll turned around and around, peering at all of them, as still as a corpse and with eyes just as lifeless. Azumi was tempted to toss it violently away, but she was overcome with a feeling that something very bad might happen if she did.

"It's a piñata," said Marcus. "Like, for a party. Someone forgot to hang them up." He searched the ceiling for hooks. "And aren't piñatas filled with things? Candy and toys and stuff like that?"

Dash picked up the one that looked like him and shook it. Azumi heard something shift inside, like sand sliding through an hourglass.

"I've never played with a piñata before," said Azumi.

"You don't play with them," said Poppy. "You break them."

"I don't want to break anything," said Dash, turning to Dylan. "I just want to get out of here."

To everyone's surprise, Poppy grabbed the doll that resembled her and twisted its arm. Its elbow snapped, and its wrist and hand dangled loosely. Marcus gasped, as if she'd done the same to him.

"What are you doing?" asked Dylan.

"I wanted to see what was in it." Poppy glanced apologetically at the rest of the group. She turned the figure and joggled it. *Swiff. Swiff. Swiff.* The group watched as a gritty gray material poured from the hole in the figurine's arm and wafted slightly around them like smoke. Most of it formed a small mound on the rug by Poppy's sneakers.

Waving the cloud away and covering her mouth and nose with her T-shirt, Poppy placed the figurine on the sofa and then leaned down and pinched a bit of the pile between her thumb and forefinger. It turned her fingertips a dark gray. "Ashes," she said.

"We all fall down," Marcus whispered with an awkward smile. No one laughed.

"What a sick joke," said Azumi.

Just then, Dylan's pocket buzzed and a muffled chime sounded. Everyone stepped away from him, as if a bomb were about to detonate.

CHAPTER 12

PULLING OUT HIS phone, Dylan was surprised to see words glowing on the screen. *You have a new voice mail!* He showed the group.

"Weird," Dash said. "The phone didn't even ring."

"But see!" said Dylan. "They're looking for us. There's just been a mix-up or something." He put the phone on speaker, pressed play, and held up the device so everyone could hear.

At first he heard only static. Then a muffled voice spoke, low and gravelly like a whisper from a person who was very ill. ". . . pleased to see you . . ." Dylan thought he could make out some background noise. ". . . games begin . . .," the voice went on. "The library."

The message ended with a series of clicking noises and what sounded like growling, followed by silence. Dylan hit the button to call back and let Del know that they were on their way, but there was still no cell service.

"That didn't sound like your great-aunt," Azumi whispered to Poppy.

Poppy blushed. "Maybe she has a deep voice?" The others were quiet for a moment.

Dylan shrugged. "Did you check *your* phone? Maybe you got a message too."

"I don't have a phone," said Poppy. Her face went scarlet. "I mean, I lost it on the way here."

"Uh-huh," said Dylan. Dash glared at him.

A hush filled the room. The dolls stared up at everyone from the floor.

"Well, let's find this library," said Dylan. "Sounds like that's where Del will be."

"Anyone have a map of this place?" Marcus chuckled.

"Yeah," said Dylan. "I picked one up at the visitor's desk on the way in." Dash nudged his brother's shoulder, warning him to bring it down a notch. Dash was always doing that, checking him. Dylan felt a flare of resentment, and he jerked himself away from his brother. "If we split up I bet we'll find it pretty quickly."

"Quick?" said Azumi. "What'll be quick about it? This place is a palace."

Dylan smiled at her, but his resentment grew. "Yeah, I can see that. We'll meet back here in like twenty minutes."

Dash spoke up. "I don't know, Dylan. How's your head feeling?"

"How many times do I have to say *I'm fine* before you get it?" Dylan snapped.

"I just thought maybe you and me could head outside and try to get some reception—"

"Stop! Seriously, chill out. Del said he'll meet us in the library."

Dash flinched. "I'm sorry. It's just—"

Azumi stepped between them. "*I* didn't hear anyone say anything about meeting anyone anywhere."

Dylan frowned. "Me and Poppy will try upstairs where we saw that kid earlier. He was probably heading to the set."

"Uh . . . okay?" said Poppy.

"And who knows, maybe phone service is better the higher up we go. I might even be able to call Del back."

"Azumi and I can search together," said Marcus. "We're both looking for the school people anyway. We'll check out the rest of the ground floor." Azumi nodded in agreement, as if happy to be away from Dylan.

"What about me?" asked Dash.

Dylan smirked. "You stay by the stairs in the foyer, in case someone comes by. That way, you don't have to worry about wandering around a big creepy house."

"But—"

Dylan held up a hand. "Someone should stay with our stuff anyway. It might as well be you."

Dash clenched his jaw. "Fine," he growled. "But if you feel weird, or dizzy, or *anything*, come right back to me. Okay?"

"Whatever you say, little brother." Dylan was already heading out of the room.

CHAPTER 13

"HELLO?" POPPY CALLED out, her small voice sounding surprisingly loud in the second floor's snaking hallway. "Anyone there?" Together, she and Dylan tried the knob on every door they passed. Some were locked, but the ones that were open didn't seem to be remarkable, except they looked old—sitting rooms, reading rooms, parlors, closets—and otherwise empty.

"I really like your show," she said as they turned another corner, the daylight fading behind them. "Scoots is kind of my favorite."

"Gosh, I hate that name." Dylan sniffed, keeping his eyes forward. "I'm actually glad to be done with it."

Poppy blushed, afraid that she'd offended him. "Oh, no! It didn't get canceled, did it?"

"Me and Dash quit. Filmed our last episode just a few days ago. It wasn't working out anymore."

"I think I remember reading about you guys on some blog recently." She tried to remember the article. "Maybe it was about this movie?"

One room was filled with filing cabinets and a couple of desks. It reminded Poppy of Ms. Tate's office at Thursday's Hope. She noticed a charcoal sketch hanging on the wall. Something about it was familiar, but she was so overwhelmed to be standing next to *the* Scooter Underwood, she couldn't remember what.

"Nothing in there," said Dylan. He paused. "Leaving the show wasn't that big of a deal, actually. It was time for a change. That's why me and Dash are here. On to bigger and better things."

"Right." Poppy listened as their footsteps creaked on the wooden floor, sending tiny shrieks out into the passages. "But I mean, you're going to miss it, right? Being in a family like that—"

"That wasn't our family," Dylan interrupted, turning toward her. "They were just a bunch of actors, working for a paycheck. And most of them were jerks anyway. They barely ever blinked at me and Dash."

"Then you did a really good job of making it seem like you all were close," she said, choosing her words carefully. "I . . . I've never had a family. So watching your show sort of made me feel like I was part of it. When you guys laughed, I laughed with you."

Dylan stared at her for a moment. "Wow. That's . . . That's really just . . . *Wow*."

Poppy felt her cheeks burn. "All I mean is, it was just, like, fun. You know? Funny."

"Yeah, real funny. So what kind of a person doesn't have a family?" he asked as he continued down the shadowed hall.

"What *kind* of a person?" Poppy echoed, her stomach squirming. She asked herself that all the time. What was it about her that made her unwanted? "Lots of people don't have families. Not traditional families anyway. Not like the ones you see on television. I lived in a group home with a bunch of other girls. Some of them were orphans. Others had parents who weren't able to care for them. My mom . . . Well, she kind of took off when I was little. That's how I ended up at Thursday's Hope."

"Jeez, that's harsh," said Dylan. He wasn't even looking at her. "So it must have been really exciting when you heard from your great-aunt."

"Yeah. Of course. Like a dream come true. And now we're going to find her."

Poppy paused, and decided to return to safer topics. "It must be so cool to work with your twin," she offered.

Dylan scoffed. "Dash can be a real pain sometimes."

There was something about his dimples that was really starting to annoy Poppy. "Do you have any clue how lucky you are to have a brother?"

"Yeah, but Dash is just . . ." Dylan stopped and looked at her. "You have no idea how weird he is."

"He really seems to care about you."

"People really care about *him*, that's for sure." Dylan started off down the hall again.

"What do you mean?"

"I mean . . . people are always saying, 'Oh, Dylan, why can't you be more responsible? Why can't you be more like Dash?' But they don't know him! They don't know how far he's willing to take things, how nasty he can really be. *I'm* not the bad twin." Dylan's voice had risen, and he dragged in a shuddering breath, as if surprised at his own outburst. He pressed his fingers against his temples. "I just think people will be really surprised when it comes to the two of us," he finished quietly.

Poppy stopped walking.

"What?" asked Dylan.

"That's an awful thing to say about your brother."

Dylan folded his arms. "I'm sorry. I should have realized you were another Dash fangirl."

Poppy shook her head. "You're not who I thought you were. You seem so *nice* on TV, so I guess you're a way better actor than anyone thought. I feel bad for your brother." She felt herself trembling. "I feel bad for *you*."

She had a small flash of satisfaction as Dylan's jaw dropped.

"I'm going to go back," Poppy said. "I want to check out that office again."

"I'll come with you."

"No, I can do it myself. *You* can leave me alone."

Dylan shrugged and stomped away.

Poppy almost called him back, but she clamped her mouth shut. She was used to doing things on her own, anyway. Still, the hall felt very empty without Dylan there. Something strange was happening here at Larkspur. Something she couldn't put into words.

She turned around and made her way to the office once again.

Poppy approached the small frame hanging on the wall by the door. Upon closer inspection, she could see that the image inside the frame was a sketch of five children. Three boys and two girls. Each face was grim, eyes hollow and empty-looking.

The children were wearing stiff dark flannel and starchy white cotton uniforms, the boys in shorts and the girls in skirts. It looked as though they had all attended the same private school fifty or sixty years prior.

Maybe Marcus and Azumi are right! Poppy thought. The style of the drawing was also familiar to her, and she suddenly remembered why. The Girl in the mirrors had given her a similar drawing—the one that Ashley had threatened to crush. Only in that other drawing, the children had been wearing masks.

The longer Poppy stared at the picture on the wall, the more suffocated she felt by her own skin. Here was proof that her oldest friend, the phantom Girl who'd attacked her earlier that morning, the Girl in the mirrors, was connected to Larkspur House.

"Delphinia, where are you?" Poppy whispered.

CHAPTER 14

DYLAN FUMED AS he continued his search for the library and Del. He couldn't believe the nerve of that girl, Poppy. The way she'd spoken to him about his brother, as if watching them on television meant she knew the *real* them. *I'm glad she wanted us to split up*, he told himself. *She doesn't know anything. She doesn't know that I'm*—The thought stopped cold, as if a door had slammed on it.

The hallway twisted deeper into the house, farther away from the daylight. When Dylan came around a sharp bend, the darkness almost seemed to reach for him. Scrambling for his phone, he held it up and switched on the flashlight. The pale beam shone only a few feet ahead, as if the shadows were denser here. As if they were alive. He scanned the walls for a light switch, but there was nothing except for iridescent-blue-patterned wallpaper, edging off into blackness.

As Dylan checked his phone for service again, he heard something moving in the distance. It sounded like the clink of metal against metal. "Del?" he called. "That you?"

A dim figure appeared from the well of shadows, walking slowly toward him. Dylan squinted. Was its face strangely shaped, or was it a trick created by the dark?

The light of his phone caught the figure, and Dylan saw it was another kid wearing a mask. A boy with the face of a bear. Black eyeholes watched him, as if there were nothing behind the mask but an unending void.

Dylan's skin prickled in the sudden chill that surrounded him. The boy wore metal cuffs around his ankles, joined by a short length of rusted chain.

A sharp pain blasted the back of Dylan's skull, and his eyes watered. His vision blurred, his body tingled as it had during the flash on the staircase, and once again, the world around him seemed to fade into something from a distant memory.

He was shoved back to the dressing room again, on the set of the show. And it was dark, darker than the shadows of Larkspur. His head felt like it had been sliced open with a blunt blade, and when he touched his scalp, a warm and sticky liquid pulsed over his fingers. He tried to yell out, but his lips wouldn't work. He realized then that he was soaking wet, and it wasn't only the blood. He stepped forward, searching for a lamp that was just out of reach. And then Dash rushed at him, coming from the dark side of the room, his face a mask of fear more terrifying than any bear or rabbit could ever be.

And then Dylan's vision cleared. The pain was gone and he was back in the hallway at Larkspur House. He slumped and then used the closest wall to catch himself. The boy in the bear mask watched.

"H-help me." The words had spilled from Dylan's mouth before he could stop them. The bear boy stepped back, cringing away from him.

Dylan shook his head, trying to clear the strange weakness away. If this kid was part of the horror film's cast, Dylan couldn't have him spreading rumors to everyone else before they even met him. Dylan stumbled toward the boy to catch him. "Hold on a second." He took a breath. "I'm fine. I'm looking for Del."

But the boy turned and ran. So Dylan lurched after him. The hallway went on and on, impossibly long. Dylan's phone light caught the slightest glimpse of the boy's chains as they rattled and shook. "Wait up!" Dylan called. "I need to talk to you!"

Ahead, the figure darted to the right. Dylan raced to the spot where the hallway turned. He could make out a thin stair-case rising up into the darkness. At the top of the stairs a door swung shut, the click of the handle echoing toward him like a period at the end of a very long sentence.

Dylan took the steps two by two. When he reached a landing, he grasped the doorknob and pulled. The door gave a couple of inches, but then something pulled back from the other side. "Hey," Dylan said, yanking on the door with all of his weight, "I didn't mean to scare you. I just want to—"

The door released, and Dylan fell backward with such force, he slid on his back a few inches along the runner, stopping just on the edge of the steps. His phone had fallen facedown somewhere nearby, and the landing was nearly pitch black.

Something stepped from the doorway.

Clink. Clink. Clink.

The metal cuffs rattled softly. Hushed breath sounded right above Dylan's face.

Huhh. Huhh. Huhh.

Dylan was suddenly too frightened to move. The boy came closer, the wooden floor creaking underneath Dylan's spine.

Dylan closed his eyes, hoping to make himself invisible. There was no way this boy was part of the film production. So why was he here at Larkspur? And why was he wearing a mask?

The breathing came closer still, inches now from Dylan's nose.

Reflexively, Dylan swung his arms up to push the boy away. But his hands didn't meet a body. Instead, they passed through air—very cold air. Dylan sat up, flattening himself against the wall as the sound of chains scrambled away, and the nearby door slammed shut again with a wild *wham!*

Dylan frantically patted along the floor until he found his phone and then shone the light toward the end of the landing.

The door was gone.

Dylan blinked. *The door was gone.*

Where the frame and the dark wood and the metal knob had been, there was only a wall covered in that Gothic blue-patterned wallpaper.

This must be a trick, he thought. The whole thing had to have been a trick. Dylan had played enough of them on other people to know when he was being messed with.

Dizzy, Dylan struggled to stand. For a moment, his scalp stung, and he worried that the horrible vision in his dressing room was about to return again. But he focused on the wall and the feeling went away.

His hands shook as he approached the spot where the door had been. His phone light fluttered. If this was a trick, he wondered, then why was his heart kicking out of his chest?

Dylan made himself touch the wall where the door had been. Then he knocked. It was solid. Glancing around, he searched for a seam or a crack, anything to indicate some sort of purposeful illusion, like something out of a magician's stage show. But there was nothing.

He turned and leaned against the wall, shining his light back down the small staircase. Maybe the boy had slipped away. Maybe he was waiting for him down there, just around the corner. Maybe—

The wall seemed to give under his weight, to soften like a pillow, calling him to sleep, luring his body down for a night of dreaming. Dylan leapt away and stared at the wall. To his horror, he could see his own silhouette pressed into the wallpaper, as if it were a wax mold instead of a wall. The shape almost looked like a shadow of himself—or maybe the boy in the mask— yearning for Dylan to return, as if it were hungry for another, longer embrace.

Dylan turned and raced down the steps, refusing to look back even as the sound of a clicking latch and the squeal of hinges reverberated past him into the dark hallway and the unseen spaces beyond.

CHAPTER 15

"**WHAT WOULD A** private school need with all this old stuff?" asked Azumi as they strolled past yet another elegant sitting room. "And where are the classrooms?" She and Marcus had seen countless fireplaces, each made out of a different material—stone, marble, brick. Their mantelpieces held hurricane lamps with bulbous glass sconces, frames filled with antique photographs, and little porcelain animals. Paintings hung on the walls—portrait after portrait of important-looking figures in elegant costumes, as well as several ethereal landscapes of the Hudson River valley. But they hadn't seen anything that looked like a school.

"Maybe it's all to impress visitors," Marcus suggested. "Like for when parents come to see what they're spending their money on." He was keeping quiet about his scholarship. He had never seen a house that looked this luxurious before, not even at the Oberlin campus where he'd performed, and he couldn't believe he was going to get to stay here. He held his hands tightly to keep from drumming the Musician's rhythm. Thankfully, Azumi didn't seem to notice.

"This is more like it," said Azumi, stepping through a doorway into an immense kitchen with numerous cupboards and cabinets. An island in its center looked like an enormous carving block that had been stained dark over the years. "Looks big enough to feed several classrooms of kids."

Marcus opened one of the cabinets. "Yes!" He pulled out a few metal trays. "Check it out." He showed Azumi the Larkspur insignia engraved in the center of each—the same little bird that had been carved into the pillars by the gate. "We're not crazy. This is definitely a school."

"But where is everybody?" asked Azumi, tugging at a drawer crammed with beat-up silverware.

Marcus opened a door beside an industrial-size refrigerator. "Hey! There's good stuff in here. Hungry?"

Azumi cracked a smile. "A little bit, actually."

"We're in luck, then." Marcus stepped aside. Through the doorway, a huge pantry was stocked with boxes of cookies and crackers, cans of tuna and tins of sardines, jars of pickles and preserves. Marcus tore open a bag of potato chips. "Tastes pretty fresh."

Azumi slid her finger under the flap of a box of chocolate wafers. Nibbling one of the cookies, she closed her eyes and sighed. "These are amazing. The only thing that might make them better is a cup of my baaba's sencha tea."

"Your *baaba*?"

"My grandmother. She lived with us for years before she died."

Marcus spoke quickly to cover the awkward pause. "We should bring some of this for when we meet up with the others again."

Azumi nodded. Together, they helped themselves, leaning against the shelves, filling their empty stomachs. After such a weird morning, it felt nice to do something as normal as a snack break.

"Where are you from again?" Marcus asked.

"Outside of Seattle," said Azumi after swallowing a graham cracker.

"So, why are you here?" Marcus asked.

Azumi squinted at him. "I already told you. For school."

"I mean, it's so far away from home."

"We're not that close to Ohio either." Azumi opened another door off the pantry, revealing several rows of long dining tables.

High windows near the ceiling allowed daylight to spill inside. "Look. This must be the dining hall."

Marcus was still looking at her. "I came here for music though. I just thought maybe you'd want to be closer to your family. There have got to be good schools on the West Coast. No?"

Azumi passed quickly through the room to an open door on the other side. "My family's a little strange right now."

"Strange how?" Marcus watched Azumi's face turn red and he felt bad for asking. He hurried after her.

Now they were in a laundry. There was a washer and dryer against the far wall, big enough to climb inside. Uniforms hung from silver racks all around the edges of the room—more evidence that they were on the right track. The insignia they'd found marked on the kitchen trays was also embroidered on a bunch of gray sweater-vests. "I'm sorry," he said. "That was really personal."

"It's okay," Azumi said, but she didn't look at him. "We lost my big sister last year."

"Oh my gosh. That's horrible." Marcus didn't know what to say. He reached out as if to hug her, then awkwardly dropped his hands. "What happened?" he asked.

"I really don't like to talk about it." Azumi shook her hair off her shoulders. "But . . . *whatever.* If we're going to be together at

Larkspur, you're going to find out eventually. My sister was being an idiot. She went off into the woods behind my aunt's house in Japan. And she disappeared. I had to come back to the States all by myself." She spoke flatly, as if she were talking about what she had for dinner last night.

"That's horrible!" Marcus said. Azumi was looking at him steadily, but he could feel the tension inside her. He felt that if he touched her, she might actually pop like a balloon. Better to change the subject? "My mom doesn't like it when I practice cello or piano," he said. The familiar tune drifted through his mind again. "She doesn't say so, but I know it bugs her. So I get mad at her sometimes. And my brothers and sister are always around, making noise, interrupting me. They hate when I put on Phillip Glass or my jazz albums. They only like 'songs with words.' Sometimes, I wish they'd *just disappear* too."

Azumi's mouth dropped open. For a moment, Marcus regretted his words. But then she released a loud laugh that reverberated around the laundry room. After a moment, she pulled herself together. "That's probably the worst thing anyone has ever said to me," she told him.

"I didn't mean . . . It came out all wrong."

"You don't really know how to talk to people, do you?"

Marcus crossed his arms, tapping his fingers on his biceps. He struggled to steady his nervous breath. "I never thought about it before. But yeah. I guess *music* is how I talk. It's how I think. Kids at my old school called me a nerd a lot."

"That's not necessarily something to be ashamed of," said Azumi. Marcus sighed in relief. "C'mon. Let's keep looking around before it gets too late. Someone's got to be around here somewhere."

Across the hallway, they discovered the biggest jaw-dropper of all—a ballroom so immense, the white ceiling overhead almost looked like the sky. A line of glass doors stretched across the far wall, covered by gauzy curtains that allowed light to filter in. "I'm pretty sure my entire house would fit in here," said Marcus.

"Mine too," said Azumi. "This is really beyond huge."

"But look!" Marcus pointed toward a far corner. A large black piano stood, its cover open wide, as if it had been waiting for him. His heart gave a great leap and he ran to it, settling himself on the bench and lifting the fallboard. He dragged his fingers silently across the keys and closed his eyes. He pressed down and a chord sang out, ringing through the chamber like church bells. Finally, he was able to release the tune that had haunted him all morning.

Azumi couldn't believe what she was hearing. Standing in the doorway of this new room, she watched Marcus move his fingers across the piano's gleaming keyboard. A beautifully complicated melody filled the space and spilled out into the hallway behind her.

Marcus had been transported to another realm. It looked like the jitters she'd seen on him had evaporated away. Gone were his shaky hands and drumming fingers. Gone were the grimaces that made him look like he was trying to block out imaginary voices in his head. He was amazing. And if he was a nerd, Azumi knew he was the best kind of nerd. The music washed over her skin like warm water, rinsing away all the bad feelings that had accumulated since her arrival at Larkspur that morning. She could have stood there and listened to him forever.

And she might have done just that if she hadn't suddenly heard a voice calling her name from somewhere down the hallway just outside the door.

"*Azuuuumi.*"

It was long and drawn out, as if coming from very far away. Azumi's body tensed. She moved away from the ballroom and stared into the murky distance of the corridor. Then she looked back at Marcus. He was so wrapped up in his melodies that he didn't even lift his head.

"Poppy?" Azumi called back. "Is that you?" But she knew that it wasn't. It was the voice she heard in her dreams, the one that had drawn her outside to the forest behind her house. It was Moriko's voice.

Azumi shut her eyes tight, hoping that when she opened them she'd be lying in her bed back home, this entire trip a dream. She wouldn't even mind if she were to open her eyes and discover herself to have been sleepwalking again, standing in the woods in the night. But when Azumi's eyes finally fluttered open, she was only deeper down the corridor, farther from Marcus's comforting melody.

Tied to a doorknob was a fluorescent-pink nylon ribbon. Just like the one Moriko had followed into the woods. Just like the one Azumi had turned away from on the last day she'd seen her sister, fearing what they'd find at the end of it. It was stretched taut and disappeared into the shadows, as if someone hidden in the distance was pulling on it.

The voice came again. "*Azumi.*"

"Moriko?" Azumi called back. She couldn't help herself. She knew it was impossible that Moriko would be here, but with her heart in her throat, she stepped forward, reached out, and then clasped the pink nylon ribbon. With a determined shake of her head, she tried to brush away the fear, and allowed the ribbon to lead her farther down the hallway and into the shadows.

CHAPTER 16

UPSTAIRS, POPPY WAS in the office space.

Several landscapes hung beside the sketch of the five uni-formed children. One tall frame that stood between the door and a red-curtained window had been draped in a thin black sheet, hiding whatever image was underneath. As curious as Poppy was about the house and her family's connection to it, something deep in her brain told her to steer clear of that one.

Desks and filing cabinets filled the room. Papers and folders were stacked on various surfaces, begging to be examined. Poppy imagined herself as a detective in one of her favorite books—Harriet the Spy or Turtle from *The Westing Game*—being clever and picking up details that even adults might miss. Maybe some of Great-Aunt Delphinia's papers were here. Poppy knew she'd have to be careful not to mix anything up in case her great-aunt walked in on her.

The top page of the first pile was an itemized invoice from a grocery store in Greencliffe to be paid by *The Larkspur Home for Children*.

Larkspur had once been a group home, just like Thursday's Hope? Was it still? Great-Aunt Delphinia hadn't mentioned anything about that. Poppy swallowed. This was not a good sign.

From nearby, there came the sound of someone sighing.

"Delphinia?" Poppy asked, holding her voice steady. No one responded.

The invoice was dated from the late 1940s. Poppy flipped through a few more pages. Apparently, Larkspur hadn't just been a home, but an orphanage. She fought against tears. Was she just going to be another foster kid to Great-Aunt Delphinia? She glanced over her shoulder at the sketch by the door. Were the kids in the drawing like her—stuck in the system, waiting for a reprieve?

Then, Poppy noticed a name at the bottom of the page in her hand that sent a thrill of excitement through her. It was a signature, belonging to the orphanage's director—a man named Cyrus Caldwell. *Another Caldwell, just like me!* She couldn't wait to ask Great-Aunt Delphinia about the family tree.

Feeling almost giddy, Poppy continued combing through the stacks of paper. Most were filled with bookkeeping documents, numbers, and data about income and costs, and almost all of them had been signed by Cyrus Caldwell.

She opened a drawer in the filing cabinets and found old files about the orphans who had lived at Larkspur. There were small pictures of the children attached to the folders. Caldwell's name was all over these too.

I wonder how he's related, Poppy thought. The papers had been signed a long time ago. Could the director still be here somewhere? Either way, there were definitely relatives of hers around. Poppy almost slumped with relief. She'd started to think she might have to go back to Thursday's Hope.

Poppy continued her search through the filing cabinet, hoping to learn more about the director or her great-aunt, then turned to the desks by a long row of squat windows at the far end of the room. A single desk there was markedly different from the others. More organized. A couple of folders thick with papers rested on a green blotter. The top one had a tab that someone had written *SPECIALS* on in bright red pencil, so the word practically leapt off the manila paper.

"*Specials?*" Poppy wondered aloud, "What are *Specials?*"

Before she had time to look closer, she heard a voice murmuring somewhere nearby. Poppy glanced up from the folder, trying to pinpoint where it was coming from. It sounded like a young girl.

Turning from the desk, she realized that the room was L-shaped, and there was a section she'd overlooked before. The voice was coming from around the corner.

"Hello?" Poppy called. She closed the *SPECIALS* folder and slipped it into her bag.

As she walked toward the voice, she could make out some of the girl's whispered words: ". . . *the bread crumbs through the forest* . . ." When Poppy was very young, the story of Hansel and Gretel had given her nightmares. It had never been the witch in the candy house who had frightened her, but instead the parents who'd heartlessly sent their children into the woods to die.

Holding her breath, Poppy peered around the bend. The midday sun shone brightly onto a single high-backed chair that faced the windows. The chair was so tall, she couldn't see the girl who was sitting there.

"Gretel didn't waste a moment," the voice continued. Poppy's shyness suddenly returned. She locked her knees and pressed her bag to her side. "She pushed the old witch into the oven, slammed the door shut, and then turned the latch, locking her in. A howl filled the cottage with a rage nearly hot enough to melt the candy walls! 'Tell me, missus,' said Gretel, smiling, 'is the oven hot enough to cook meat now?' Then she turned toward the cage made of bones where her brother had crouched, watching her with both wonder and terror."

The room fell silent, and Poppy's skin prickled. "Hello?" she called again.

The person in the high-backed chair shifted, the chair swiveled around slowly, and Poppy found herself staring into the blank eyes of a girl in a light-gray cat mask. She flinched with surprise. On the mask, the cat's eyebrows were lifted high, as if Poppy shouldn't have dared interrupt the fairy tale.

Poppy tried again. "Um, do you live here? Can you help me find Delphinia?"

Poppy trembled. She recognized the cat from the charcoal sketch that Ashley had almost destroyed. The girl in the chair also wore the familiar dark skirt, white blouse, and gray sweater. Long brown hair fell from the top of her head, a few stray strands caught in the edges of the mask's eyeholes.

But this couldn't be the *same* girl from the drawing, could it? And why wasn't she saying a word?

On the floor by the wall sat the girl's audience—a group of dolls propped up against the baseboard. All of them were damaged in some way. Disfigured. Some of them were burnt, their faces mottled and blackened. Others were missing limbs and blank-eyed. One of the larger ones was slumped over

with a smashed head, a gaping hole in its fragile porcelain skull.

The girl in the cat mask followed Poppy's gaze down to the pile of dolls for a moment before whipping her head back toward Poppy.

"I'm sorry," said Poppy, horrified that some of her revulsion might have shown on her face. She knew better than most what strange things could become treasures. "I—"

But then the girl stood and Poppy retreated into silence. The girl bent down, gathered up her dolls, then stepped toward Poppy, her eyeholes black and empty. "*You came,*" said the girl, her muffled voice the perfect combination of Gretel and the witch. "*You actually came.*"

"Wait! Are you the one who invited me?" Poppy asked, her voice barely a whisper, her heart pounding.

The girl emitted a low laugh that went on for a long time. Then, suddenly, she shrieked. The noise was so unexpected that it startled Poppy into a strangled scream too. The girl kicked the high-backed chair away with startling force. It fell to the floor with a hard whack. Then she stepped toward Poppy again.

Poppy backed around the corner. She was enveloped by a strong smell of smoke, and for a moment she imagined that it had followed her out of the girl's story, as if heat from the witch's oven had become magically real. But then hot air breezed against her back. A moment later, bright, flickering flame burst to light behind her.

Poppy screamed in earnest now. The office was ablaze.

CHAPTER 17

ALL OF THE desks and cabinets, the folders and files that Poppy had just searched, erupted into flame. The fire climbed the walls, turning the wallpaper black and the paintings crisp and crackling. In the furious heat, the black cloth that had covered the tallest frame rose up in a hot gust and then slid to the floor, where the fire devoured it, revealing an enormous mirror. Poppy briefly thought of the Girl right before the mirror's glass fractured with a *crack* as loud as a gunshot, creating a spiderweb of breaks that stretched across its tarnished surface.

For a moment, Poppy knew she had to be imagining everything. *There is no fire*, she thought. *There is no cat girl. This is all in your head. You really are crazy. They're going to lock you in a dark room forever and ever. No friends. No family. No mirrors or books. Just you and your stupid, crazy brain.*

Then something grabbed hold of her hair and yanked. Poppy fell backward with a scream and landed on the floor. The cat-faced girl stared down at her. Above the crackling of the flames, it sounded as if she was laughing.

This was real.

Poppy scrambled away and leapt to her feet.

The blaze was closing in on the two of them. "What are you DOING?!" Poppy yelled at the cat-faced girl. Poppy ran across the room, leaping over small licks of flame. But when she yanked on the knob, the door wouldn't budge.

"NO!" she screamed. "Help!"

Smoke obscured the room behind her, shrouding the cat-faced girl in swirling gray. Fire swelled into the room and the heat grew stronger.

Poppy struggled to inhale, but the heat seared her throat and she choked. Out of nowhere, Ms. Tate blinked into her head, standing before the girls in the common area at Thursday's Hope, instructing them on what to do in case of a fire. *Get low to the ground to avoid the smoke*. Poppy dropped to her knees, covering her mouth. *Know your closest exits*.

Exits. Poppy forced herself to think.

There was a window next to the broken mirror! The red velvet curtain was roaring with flames, but the glass was clear.

Poppy grabbed the metal chair at the desk. It was hot to the touch, but she gritted her teeth against the pain. She raised it above her head and threw it as hard as she could at the window. A perfect shot. But to her horror, the chair simply bounced away.

"Dylan!" she screamed, coughing, sweat running down her face and neck, drenching her T-shirt. "Marcus! Azumi! Help me!" The fire was so loud now, the blood pounding so hard in her eardrums, that even if any of them answered, she wouldn't hear them.

The smoke across the room seemed to part like a veil. A figure stepped into the flames—the girl in the cat mask. Poppy froze, unsure again if her eyes were playing tricks. The fire seemed to dance *around* the cat girl. The girl walked slowly forward, clutching her collection of monstrous dolls and staring at Poppy with malice.

"You don't scare me!" Poppy shouted. She hated that her voice sounded so trembling and weak.

The girl tilted her head as if to ask, *Don't I?* She glided slowly through the growing flames toward the spot where Poppy crouched.

You came. You actually came.

The wallpaper beneath the sketch of the masked five was bubbling. Smoke and steam billowed out from the seams, and

Poppy gagged at the fumes. The fire was inside the wall now. Soon, it would rush to the upper and lower floors. Poppy knew the entire structure could collapse.

Know your closest exits.

A fierce anger filled her, the same anger that had made her search for her file in Ms. Tate's office. *If there's no way out, make one.*

Poppy stared into the shattered mirror. Her reflection was a fractured, frightening mess, but it wasn't her reflection she was looking for. "You were trying to warn me not to come here," she yelled to the Girl, *her* Girl, Poppy's voice barely audible over the roar of the fire. "I'm sorry I didn't listen. But please, *please*, if you can hear me, help me!"

The cat girl was now only a few steps away. She held out her dolls, as if to taunt Poppy with what was about to happen.

If there's no way out, make one.

A slight flicker moved inside the broken mirror.

The Girl! She'd come!

The mirror fractured again. A horizontal line broke through the web pattern over Poppy's reflection. Then two more cracks formed on either side of Poppy's face. Turning around, Poppy saw the fissures cracking through the wall she was huddled against. The cracks in the mirror were duplicating themselves on the wall behind her.

The girl in the cat mask howled as Poppy slammed her weight against the wall. When Poppy drew back and hit it with her shoulder again, the wall swung open like a gate.

A moment later, Poppy had collapsed out into the hallway. Inside the burning room, the mirror exploded, shards of broken glass hurtling into the fire. The passage through the wall disappeared with a blink, and Poppy found herself staring at an unblemished hallway.

Poppy leaned back, gasping for breath. She closed her eyes, then opened them and looked again. Nothing. And no burns on her, no hint of smoke.

Craazzy Poppy.

Slamming her palms against the wall behind her, Poppy shoved the taunting voices away. But that only left her with her own voice ringing in her head, and she didn't know if she liked that any better.

This is all a lie. The letter. The invitation. Great-Aunt Delphinia.

Something had wanted Poppy to come to Larkspur, but it hadn't been some long-lost family member. This place wasn't going to be her home. No one here was going to accept her, love her, adopt her.

She fought against the rising flood of tears, her eyes red and prickling. Poppy felt like one of the dolls that the girl in the cat mask had been telling a story to, the one that had been gutted, its stuffing removed. She struggled to stay on her feet and angrily wiped her face clean.

Then Poppy heard the sound of footsteps racing toward her.

CHAPTER 18

POPPY FACED THE footsteps, swinging her satchel from her shoulder and holding it hard in her hands like a weapon—until she saw the face of the person rushing toward her. She was so relieved, she nearly dropped her bag.

"Dylan!" she cried out.

"Nope," said the boy. "But close." His eyes were wide, and his chest was heaving.

"Dash? What are you doing up here?"

"Where's my brother?" Dash looked almost as scared as she felt.

"We decided to split up." She glanced over her shoulder toward the office door. "We need to find the others and then get out of here."

"You saw something too?"

Nodding, Poppy fought tears.

This is all a lie.

"I was waiting in the foyer," said Dash, "just like Dylan told me to. But I heard a noise. When I turned, I saw that kid in the rabbit mask watching me from the top of the stairs. He ran off, so I followed him up here—"

"I don't know what's going on." Poppy couldn't hold back. "I was in an office. There was a fire. A girl in a cat mask attacked me. I thought she was going to kill me. I ran, but the door was locked. And the window wouldn't break. But the wall . . . The fire went out, which makes no sense . . . And . . . And we have to go." She shifted past him, waving for him to follow. "We have to find the others *AND GO.*"

"Not that way," he said.

"What do you mean?" She heard her voice rising. "The stairs are just down the hall."

Dash turned his head to show her the nasty welt on his cheek. Poppy hissed in shock and sympathy. "The kid I followed attacked me too. I managed to pull off his mask." Dash trembled and briefly closed his eyes. "There was black goo spilling out of his mouth and down his neck. He was soaked with it." He swallowed. "I don't want—I don't think we should go back that way."

Poppy met his eyes gravely. "The stairs are back that way. I haven't seen another way out."

Dash peered past her into the darkness stretching down the hallway behind her. "Fine. But if we come across another one of those kids wearing masks, I hope you know how to fight."

"I'm learning," said Poppy, leading the way, relieved to finally put some distance between herself and that office.

Moments later, not far down the hall, they came upon the rabbit mask lying on the floor, lit by sunlight from an open doorway.

It wasn't anything elaborate, just a thin sheet of plastic that had been pressed by a mold at a factory somewhere. But the eyes were wide and dark, their edges marked with deep laugh lines. In the pale light from the nearby doorway, they looked hollow, black. The mouth was stretched in a wide and grotesque smile, with a tiny slit cut in the plastic so its wearer could breathe. There were dried black flecks spattered around this small hole.

"You sure you want to touch that?" Poppy asked as Dash reached for it.

Dash glanced at her. "We can't just leave it here. The others won't believe my story." Poppy understood what he'd meant: *Dylan* won't believe my story. Dash turned the mask over. The bottom half was dripping with black goo.

Poppy gasped and covered her mouth. "Ugh. Nasty!"

"Never mind," Dash said, and dropped it, wiping his hands on his shorts.

Poppy noticed red markings on the inside of the mask, higher up, closer to the rabbit's left ear. Block letters in red marker spelled out *ALOYSIUS*. "What's this?" she asked, pointing.

"I don't know and I don't want to," Dash said. "I just want to get out of here."

They continued on toward the staircase. "Dylan?" Dash called out. His voice echoed back at him, but no one answered.

As they went around the next corner, Poppy yelped. Just ahead, lying on the floor in a sunbeam, was the same rabbit mask, still looking up with its blank eyeholes. "What's going on?" she asked. *Craazzy Poppy.* "Dash, you see that too, right?"

"I don't understand," said Dash slowly. He looked close to tears. "Dylan!" He called out again. He gathered himself together and quietly said, as if to himself, "It's got to be one of Dylan's tricks. He's messing with us."

"After everything we've just seen, you think *your brother* is responsible for this?"

"I don't know what to think!" Dash yelled. "I don't even know which direction to take."

"Let's just keep going?" said Poppy, but her feet felt unsteady.

They walked on for a few minutes—far longer than it should have taken to find the staircase—and suddenly they were back in the same spot. Panic gripped Poppy's lungs, and she felt like she couldn't breathe. Dash rushed up and stomped on the rabbit mask until the plastic was smashed flat.

The hallway shuddered and groaned. Dash grabbed Poppy's hands and brought her low to the floor, as if they were bracing for an earthquake.

"It's not happy you did that," Poppy whispered.

"What's not happy?"

Poppy didn't want to say it out loud. "I don't know . . . The house?"

Inches away, the flattened rabbit mask popped back into shape.

Poppy and Dash leapt to their feet and bolted around the corner and past the rabbit mask. There, they found a new hallway, one they hadn't seen before. They ran and ran, looking for new doorways, new rooms, new details they hadn't yet encountered—anything to get them out of this strange loop.

Poppy yanked Dash to a halt. "You hear that?" she asked, her chest heaving.

"Music!"

"Someone's playing a piano."

"Let's follow it."

"But what if it's—"

"Just go!"

119

Poppy and Dash raced around a bend, and the landing at the top of the stairs finally appeared. "Yes!" she shouted, feeling like she'd just won a marathon.

Dash bolted past her, down the steps toward the foyer. "Hurry!" he shouted. Poppy didn't need him to tell her twice.

When the two of them finally made it to the bottom of the stairs, a voice called out from up above, "Dash! Wait!" Turning, they found Dylan standing on the landing, wide-eyed and unsteady. He looked like he was about to faint.

"Oh my goodness," said Poppy, shaking her head, confused. "I totally forgot Dylan was there too!"

"Help me!" said Dash. Together, Poppy and Dash raced back up the stairs toward his brother.

CHAPTER 19

MARCUS WAS LOST in an ocean of sound. The piano melody swelled as he danced his fingers across the keys and pressed his feet against the pedals. Marcus could hear the Musician's tune a millisecond before he brought it to life. It felt as if they were playing a duet. The ballroom where he sat was a hazy memory. His head was filled with pictures of home, of kind friends and family, of the scent of Duke's wet fur after a walk in the rain, of the sound of the calliope during the county fairs on Labor Day weekends, of his mother and his siblings sitting in the darkness of the auditoriums' first rows—memories that were now so entangled with the Musician's tunes that Marcus couldn't distinguish one sense from the other.

That serenity was shattered when a group burst through the ballroom doorway, shouting for his attention. Marcus lifted his hands from the keys and opened his eyes, feeling as if he'd been bumped out of a dream.

Poppy and Dash were struggling to carry Dylan between them. His arms were stretched between their shoulders, his feet practically dragging.

Marcus stood up, shocked, pushing the bench back with a squeal that mixed with the reverberation left over from his shattered melody. "What's wrong with him?"

"We don't know!" said Dash, his eyes huge with worry. "He practically fainted on the stairs again. This is all my fault!"

Dylan fell to his knees, holding his head. As the last of the echo seeped into the woodwork and faded away, he finally looked up. "I'm sorry," he said, with no trace of his former cockiness. "I don't know what happened to me."

"I told you to come find me if you felt strange!" Dash said, crouching beside him.

Dylan winced. "I didn't feel strange until I found you, so please . . . stop shouting at me."

"Where were you guys?" Marcus asked.

"Upstairs," said Poppy. "The music led us down to you."

"There are other people here," said Dylan. "Kids wearing masks. I think they're messing with us. Playing tricks." He glanced at Dash.

"You saw another one too?" asked Dash. Dylan nodded, swallowing hard, as if he were fighting nausea. Dash's mouth flattened. "The rabbit-faced boy we saw earlier attacked me. And Poppy said a cat girl came after her. We need to get out of here."

Poppy jumped in, "Upstairs, I found an old office filled with files. I think this building was an orphanage once. All the paperwork, for decades, was signed by its director. He has the same last name as me—Caldwell!"

"One more reason to just run," said Dash, edging toward the row of windows on the other side of the room. "Come on!"

"That is weird," said Marcus, crossing his arms. Kind of unbelievably weird. He wished they would leave him alone so he could sit down again at the piano and play. He wanted that warm feeling back, the pleasant memories, the safety of it all. "Maybe everyone should just calm down and talk this out. It sounds very confusing."

"But that wasn't even the weirdest part!" said Dash. "There was a fire, and Poppy got locked in the room, and then—"

"Wait," said Dylan. "There's a fire upstairs?"

"Not anymore," said Poppy. "It went out."

Marcus raised an eyebrow.

"And then," Dash went on, "when we were trying to find our way back to the foyer, the hallways kept moving."

"The hallways—" Marcus crossed his arms. "I'm sorry. That's not possible."

Dash looked at Poppy. "Am I lying?"

Poppy shook her head, blushing. She followed Dash to the line of windows.

"Do you think all of this could be part of the horror movie?" Dylan asked. His voice was low and strained.

"No!" said Dash. "And you don't either! There's something seriously wrong with this place." Dash made a beeline toward the French doors. "I am seriously creeped out. It's time to leave. I don't care *what* we all came here for."

"Agreed." Poppy exhaled on a shaky breath. "There's nothing here for any of us. My great-aunt. Marcus's school. The film shoot. It's all just . . ." She hesitated, glancing around the ballroom. "Where is Azumi?"

Marcus looked behind him. "She was just here. Wasn't she?"

"Not when we came in," Dash said. "When did you last see her?"

"I'm not sure." Marcus walked to the doorway and peered into the hall, glancing in both directions. "I was caught up playing the piano. I thought she was listening to me."

"How could you let her out of your sight?" Dylan demanded. "Were you really that wrapped up in playing a stupid piano?"

"She's a big girl!" said Marcus. "She can do what she wants!"

Poppy sighed. "Not in *this* house, she can't. Here, we're like mice in a maze."

"It's not my fault she's gone!"

Dash grabbed the handles of the French doors. "You guys can hang around waiting for Azumi, but I'm out." But when he pulled down on the handles, they wouldn't budge. He struggled for a few moments before backing away, looking for a latch or a lock that he could release.

"What about Del?" asked Dylan, coming up behind Dash.

"Didn't you hear Poppy?" Dash shouted, moving toward the piano. "She said Del doesn't exist! And I believe she's right." He dragged the piano bench several feet back toward the door.

Poppy's eyes were wide and scared. "I tried to smash a window upstairs with a chair, but it wouldn't break," she whispered.

Dash tossed it at the glass anyway. It bounced off, clattering to the floor with a raucous echo. Marcus ran back into the room, shocked.

"See?" said Poppy.

"I can't believe this." Dash tried to toss the bench several more times, but the door remained intact.

"But the email," said Dylan quietly. "The voice mail. We *heard* his voice." Nobody paid him any attention, even as he stomped his foot. "Am I invisible?"

"We came in through the front door," said Marcus. He tried forcing himself to remain calm, but the fright of the others was slowly infecting him. "We could leave that way too."

"I don't think it'll be any different," said Poppy. She seemed to be fighting against tears again.

"How would we even find our way back there?" asked Dash.

Marcus shrugged. "By going to look for it."

"You didn't see what we saw upstairs," said Dash. "The hallways were moving! The whole house keeps changing shape." The group stared at Dash for a moment. "If it doesn't want us to leave, I don't think we can."

"What do you mean *if it doesn't want us to leave*?" said Dylan. "How can a house not want us to leave?"

"We have to find Azumi before we do anything else," said Poppy, heading toward the hallway. "Right? I mean, maybe she'll already have found a way out."

"Let's try for the front door," said Marcus evenly. "Maybe we'll run into Azumi. We can figure out what to do from there."

"I already know what we can do from there," said Dash, making his way back across the room in a huff. "We can go." He took his brother's arm and disappeared into the hallway.

CHAPTER 20

MARCUS SHOOK HIS head at Poppy and followed the twins. "Me and Azumi found a whole bunch of stuff that made it pretty clear this place is a *school*. A boarding school, like with uniforms and a big kitchen with silverware and food trays and . . . and a pantry with enough food to feed an entire—"

"Orphanage?" Poppy interrupted, her voice growing higher. "That doesn't sound so different from a boarding school. I mean, right? That was what I found upstairs. Files and files and files." Poppy blinked and gathered herself. Ahead, Dash and Dylan were rushing side by side down the hallway. The light at the end of the hallway looked familiar. Hopefully it was coming from the grand foyer. "Please tell me we're all thinking the same thing," she said quietly. "I don't want to feel like the one weirdo here."

"And what should we all be thinking?" asked Dylan over his shoulder.

"That Larkspur is haunted," said Poppy. "The girl that I saw *walked through fire*. How is that possible? And she spoke to me. She said, 'You came. You actually came,' as if she'd been expecting me! What if these kids in masks are making us see, feel, and hear things that aren't real? Or that *were* real once . . . I don't know! I have no clue how hauntings work."

All three boys stopped and stared at her, not moving, as if too frightened to agree.

Marcus touched her elbow, and Poppy flinched. "I think maybe you should find a place to sit," he said.

Poppy shook him off. "No! I've seen things before. Really strange things. And I'm beginning to wonder if those things have to do with why I'm here."

"What kind of things?" asked Dylan.

Poppy closed her eyes briefly and shook her head. "I always thought of her as if she were a friend. My only friend."

"Her *who*?" Marcus asked. Was it Poppy's imagination, or had Marcus gone pale?

"Promise you won't laugh."

"We promise," said Dash.

Poppy took a minute. She'd kept the secret clenched inside herself for so long that it was almost an effort to let it out. "A

Girl. She stands behind me whenever I look in a mirror." Poppy locked eyes with Dash. He *had* to believe her. "My whole life I've seen her. My mother . . . she left me when I was five. I grew up in a group home. So this Girl was special to me." Dash raised an eyebrow and glanced at his brother, who looked away. Poppy swallowed her nerves. "The Girl was always smiling. Always warm. Until I found my great-aunt's letter. Then she changed. In fact, when I reached Larkspur's gate, I'm pretty sure she's what grabbed me and threw me to the ground. That's where you found me, Marcus."

Marcus wouldn't look at her.

"I thought she'd turned on me," Poppy went on. "Jealous or something. But she wasn't trying to hurt me. She was trying to stop me from coming here."

Dylan looked revolted. "That's as creepy as . . . I don't even know what."

"But you believe me?"

Marcus wouldn't meet Poppy's eyes. His own Musician had gone silent for the moment, but Marcus remembered the therapist and the threat of medication. He remembered how he'd forced himself to keep the Musician a secret so that he could keep the music in his life. Marcus balled his fists. Poppy had said she didn't want to be the weirdo here; well, neither did he.

"Not really," he heard himself say. Poppy looked at him with wide, shocked eyes.

It suddenly struck Marcus that what everyone was suggesting—to leave this place, to give up on everything each of them had hoped to find here—would bring him back to Ohio, to his ordinary life where his siblings and classmates just didn't understand jazz or classical music, to his mother, who hated listening to him practice because of her memories of her dead brother. He hadn't realized until this moment how much he *needed* to stay at Larkspur, to believe that this was the music school he was always meant to attend. His Musician's tune had proven this, hadn't it? He'd never felt more truly at home as he had playing the melody on the ballroom piano.

The twins glanced at each other, unsure what to say.

Marcus went on. "Have you ever seen a doctor about these visions?"

Poppy scowled. "The Girl's not a *vision*. She's . . . It's hard to explain."

"I mean, it sounds pretty simple to me," said Marcus, hating himself. "People sometimes hallucinate."

"Was Dylan hallucinating?" Poppy asked. Her face was flaming. "Was Dash?" She turned toward the foyer and continued walking. The boys followed.

"I don't know!" Marcus shouted. "But they're not the ones who've seen imaginary girls standing behind them in mirrors their whole lives."

"I told you, she's *not* imaginary," Poppy yelled.

"Here we are!" Dash cried out as they made their way into the foyer. "The main entrance!" He raced to the solid double doors, grappling with the handles. But just like in the ballroom, the doors would not give.

"But this is how we came in," said Dylan, moving toward the tall, thin window beside the door, peering out of it. "How are they locked *now*?" He smacked the pane hard with his knuckles. There was a loud thud, and Dylan groaned. The glass did not shatter.

"This way," said Dash. The group rushed to follow him into the game room. He went for the closest window lock, but the lever wouldn't turn. None of them would.

"This is so messed up," said Dylan, grabbing the wire bingo globe off the nearby table, the plastic letters rattling inside it. It was heavy; it took two hands to arc it back behind his head and then whip it at the closest window. The globe hit it with enough force to snap a couple of wires, but the glass didn't break. The little red balls inside spilled onto the floor, rolling in all directions, looking like beads of blood. "I don't understand," said

Dylan. He moved from window to window, pounding on the glass.

"What about the door's hinges?" Poppy asked. "Can we take it apart that way?"

Dash ran back to the entry. "There are no hinges!" he called out.

"How can a door not have hinges?" asked Marcus.

"They're gone." Dash returned to the game room and threw his hands into the air. "How can *any* of this be happening?"

Poppy grabbed the back of one of the game room couches. "Maybe if we use the furniture to make some sort of battering ram . . . ?"

"A battering ram?" said Marcus, shaking his head. "This isn't a video game, Poppy."

"It was just a thought . . ."

"I don't think *anything* we do will get these doors or windows open," said Dash, his voice strained and trembling. "Poppy was right. It's this place, or those kids, or something. They wanted us here. And now they won't let us go."

A wave of cold fear grabbed at the four kids, and for a moment all they could do was stand there, shuddering, frozen in place.

CHAPTER 21

AZUMI HAD BEEN following the pink nylon ribbon down the dark and twisted corridor for so long, she almost expected to arrive back at the starting point. But she kept going and going, wandering around corners, stumbling up and down steps, without even crossing the path she'd already walked.

How big is this place? Azumi wondered.

The ribbon was starting to feel like a safety line back to the way out.

The hallway stretched about a hundred yards farther before coming to another T-shaped crossing. With her phone's flashlight, Azumi could see the nylon ribbon veer around the corner to the right. She listened to her breath, counting in her head with every exhalation so that she had something to focus on other than the growing strangeness of the situation.

Azumi didn't see the backpack on the floor until her sneaker caught on the strap, and she tripped, letting go of the ribbon and landing sprawled on the floor.

Her hand trembled as she reached for the backpack. Its blue canvas was faded, as if it had been bleached by the elements. Its front pockets had been worn through and the sides were ragged, as if torn open by hungry animals. Inside, Azumi could see what she knew were stacks of notebooks, once waterlogged but now dry. She knew that if she were to reach in, pull out one of the books, and open it to any page, she'd see ink that had bled into gray splotches, words that had been leeched away by water.

Azumi kicked the bag away hard, and it arced away from her and hit a distant wall with a satisfying smack.

This backpack had been one of the first objects that she and Moriko had stumbled upon in the forest behind Auntie Wakame's house in Yamanashi Prefecture. And here it was, waiting in Larkspur for Azumi to find it again.

Something shifted down the hallway. There was a scuffling of feet.

"Who's there?" Azumi demanded. "What is going on here?" She grabbed her phone and shone the light into the shadows. A few more objects were scattered throughout the hall in the darkness ahead of her, but from where she sat, Azumi couldn't make out what they were.

She stood slowly, waiting for the scuffling sound to come again, but the hallway was quiet. Following the ribbon, she made her way to the next object. It was a wrinkled photograph, its subjects staring up at Azumi. She knew this one too. It was a snapshot of a father standing with his daughter on the corner of a busy street, her arms slung around his neck, both of them smiling for the camera. Azumi knew it was taken in Tokyo. She also knew that if she were to flip over the photograph, she'd find kanji written on the back in ballpoint pen: *Good-bye, my lovely girl. Forgive me.* Azumi's Japanese wasn't nearly as good as her parents wanted it to be, but she'd studied this photograph before too—in the forest on the day Moriko went missing. With every discovery, she felt herself growing giddy, as if she might lose control and start laughing again, like she had done with Marcus in the laundry. She pulled her jacket tight across her middle and forced the feeling away, determined to keep hold of herself.

Azumi remembered the time last year when Moriko had tried to pierce her belly button with a sewing needle. Azumi had run to tell her parents what her sister was about to do. They'd laughed, and Azumi had fumed. "It's going to get infected!" she'd insisted.

"So then let it get infected," her father had said. "Your sister will learn, won't she?"

Let it get infected. That was the thought that had gone through Azumi's head when she headed back to Auntie Wakame's cottage on that last afternoon. Those were the words she thought of as the sun had set and she'd held her tongue about leaving Moriko alone on the path at the edge of the woods, holding on to that stupid pink ribbon. *Your sister will learn, won't she?*

Azumi had no idea at the time how that infection would spread—how it would sneak into her brain like a worm, turn her into a mindless zombie, and walk her unknowingly into the darkness of her dreams.

Coming to the end of the hallway, Azumi ran around the corner, following the ribbon. There was light up ahead coming from a doorway on the right. Pieces of paper were strewn like bread crumbs all the way into the distance. Azumi ventured on, bending down to examine these pages. Picking up several of them, she noticed that the same words were written in pencil at the top of each: *Dear Sister—*

Someone was toying with her. With all of them. The creepy papier-mâché figurines that looked like the group of kids she'd met that day and now the ribbons and things from the woods here in the house . . .

She picked up another page. This one was different. The words *Dear Azumi* were followed by a series of thick black lines, Magic Marker inked over the rest of the message. Azumi looked

136

closer. Holding the flashlight in just the right position, she was able to make out indentations in the paper, more of the message that someone had tried to erase.

Dear Azumi,
I miss you so much. If only we could see each other face to face...

A spark of anger lit in her stomach, and she had to stop herself from crumpling the page. Someone had mimicked Moriko's writing perfectly. Who would make fun of her sister like this? She hadn't told anyone about Moriko besides Marcus. Was this the type of joke that he'd try, to get back at her for whatever dumb thing she might have said earlier to offend him?

A muffled cough echoed from up ahead. A figure was standing in the pale light filtering through a doorway, holding the end of the pink ribbon. Azumi squinted. "Hello?"

The figure didn't answer her. Didn't move. Trying to keep herself from trembling, Azumi approached steadily. "Did you write this?" Azumi found herself fighting tears. "Answer me!" She didn't know what emotion she was feeling. They were all so mixed up.

She thought of the day weeks prior when she'd searched online for East Coast schools and how only one entry kept

Dear Sister,

I miss you so much. If only we could see each other face to face, I know I would finally find the comfort I've needed this past year. I know you would explain everything to me, tell me why you haven't come to find me...

I can't remember what happened anymore... One minute you were right beside me, and the next second I couldn't see you. Did the Director talk to you, too?

Why haven't I heard from you?? Have you gotten my letters? Have I even sent them, or is this just a cruel trick of my imagination, telling me that I've been waiting **and waiting** to hear from you when you have no idea where I am?

coming up. *Larkspur.* Was this person responsible for that too? It didn't seem possible. Not physically, nor emotionally—she'd never imagined that someone could be so cruel.

She was about to tear the papers to pieces, but the figure stepped into the faint beam of her flashlight and Azumi's breath was swept from her lungs.

"Moriko?" Azumi wheezed. Her face was on fire. Her skin tingled, and then the hallway tilted, or maybe it only seemed so.

The figure stepped back into the shadows, the details of her appearance melting away. She dropped the end of the ribbon and then disappeared through the doorway on her right.

"Moriko, wait!" Azumi called out. She raced after her sister.

CHAPTER 22

"HEY, OVER HERE," Dash called from up ahead. He and Dylan were standing in front of a large wooden door on the right side of the corridor. "Maybe this one leads to an exit!" The top of the door rose high over their heads, crowned in a sunburst-shaped arc. Marcus and Poppy approached the twins, and the door, cautiously. Dylan was already pulling at the doorknob.

"I don't think so," said Marcus. "Look."

Dylan hadn't noticed the dozen or more rusty nails that had been hammered along the outer edge of the door, piercing the frame around it. Frustrated, Dash pushed his brother's hands away from the knob. "It looks like someone wants to keep people out of there."

"Either that," said Poppy, "or they want to keep someone inside."

Dash closed his eyes, and Poppy realized that she should try harder to not frighten her new friends. Friends? Was that what they'd become? Despite the animosity she'd already felt building between herself and both Dylan and Marcus, she had to admit that Dash was feeling like a friend. "I'm sorry, Dash," she said. It was hard for her to say. The girls at Thursday's Hope hardly ever apologized unless Ms. Tate threatened them with punishment.

"Listen," Dylan whispered. He brought his ear close to the door but didn't touch it. The others decided they could hear just fine from where they stood. A slight scratching sound was coming from within, like long fingernails dragging along the wood. Dylan glanced at the others. "Do you think it's Azumi?" None of them wanted to call out or make their presence known.

"What if it is?" Poppy asked. "We'd need a hammer to pry those nails away."

"We could go look for one," said Marcus, but nobody appeared willing to head back into the dark passage behind them.

The doorknob rattled violently, and everyone jumped back. There was a sudden pounding, and the door itself jounced and trembled. It bulged outward and the nails in the door frame strained.

Dash whimpered. They were all too frightened to move. Too scared to speak. But Dash knew they were all thinking the same thing he was: *One of the masked kids is in there, and he or she is trying to get to us.*

Then, as suddenly as the pounding started, it stopped—the scratching too. The hallway was filled with a quiet that seemed to ring in their eardrums like a long and steady hum. No one dared to breathe. Which was strange because, all of a sudden, the echo of a stifled inhalation interrupted the silence like a knife.

"Marcus," Dylan whispered, his eyes round with terror. "Someone is standing behind you."

CHAPTER 23

EVERYONE TURNED TO LOOK.

Down the wide hallway, several yards past the door with the nails, a boy was staring back at them. Or at least he appeared to be staring—it was difficult to tell because of his mask. This one was shaped like a dog's head, its lips drawn all the way back to the boy's ears. He had shaggy blondish hair and was dressed similarly to the others they had seen that day: stiff flannel pants, a white shirt, and a gray sweater.

"Who are you?" Marcus yelled. "What do you want?"

The boy in the dog mask stepped closer to Marcus, nodding, as if taunting him. He was clutching a broken violin, holding the jagged body of the instrument in one hand. The neck dangled by the strings, swaying against the boy's leg like a metronome.

"He's just trying to scare us," said Dylan, stepping toward the boy. Dash reached out to pull him back, but Dylan shook off his grip. "Not a good idea, kid. Back up!"

"Dylan, shut your mouth," Dash pleaded through clenched teeth.

"Marcus," Poppy whispered. "You're too close!"

The boy in the mask slowly turned his head as if to acknowledge everyone's presence. Then, all at once, he swung the body of the violin forward. It smacked Marcus in the face so hard that he fell to the floor. Before anyone else could move, the masked boy hurled himself forward and pounced on Marcus, straddling his chest and stretching the strings of the broken violin across his neck to cut off his breath. Marcus's eyes went wide and he let out a strangled scream.

"Stop that!" Dash shouted. "Get off him!" He bolted forward, barreling into the attacker's side. The boy in the dog mask barely flinched, and Dash fell to the floor.

"Whoa," said Dylan. "You are *so* done." He charged, but he was too slow. With a slight feint, the boy twisted his body out of the way. He lifted his knee like a piston and brought it down on Dash's neck, pinning him beside Marcus. Dylan was too shocked to move.

"Dylan!" Dash wheezed.

"Leave them alone," shouted Poppy, throwing off her shock and flying into the fray. She yanked at the strings that were cutting into Marcus's throat. Dylan tried to kick out the boy's knee, but the boy swiveled out of the way.

"Dylan, watch it!" yelled Poppy.

The boy hissed at Dylan, flinching as Dylan swung his fist toward his head. Poppy shoved hard at the masked boy's shoulder, and Dash managed to twist his torso and then scramble out from under him.

Marcus reached up from where he was flailing on the floor. "Get . . . off . . . of us!" he gurgled, attempting to clutch at the boy's clothing to drag him off-balance.

Dylan came forward again, fists raised. He reached out and tried to grab the boy's sweater, but his hand seemed to slip right through it. The boy looked up, and the dog mask seemed to change, the eyes growing wider, the upper lip curling back in a snarl, revealing yellow plastic teeth. He bolted to his feet and then cringed, as if he were startled by Dylan's attempt to touch him.

There was a great booming sound followed by a resounding crack. The building shook, and from somewhere far away came a noise like a roar. The boy scuttled from the group, rolling toward the door with the nails, dragging his broken violin across the rug, cowering. Marcus sat up, gasping and choking.

The four kids retreated to the center of the hallway. They watched the boy in horror, their muscles coiled like springs. But the boy was fixated on the wall behind them. Turning, they discovered a wide, jagged opening staring back. It hadn't been there moments earlier. The booming sound, the cracking noise, the roar . . . The house had changed shape around them again.

At the far end of this dark and dusty passageway, a light blinked on. A small chandelier globe in the ceiling of a brass elevator cage.

The boy in the dog mask groaned and shifted against the far wall. He clutched his broken violin close to his chest and was watching them intently now, as if he'd forgotten the fear that had distracted him from his anger. Deep in his esophagus, his voice rattled wordlessly: *Ehrrrrr.*

Dash jumped to his feet, clutching at his throat. "We need . . ." He struggled to catch his breath. "We need to get away from here." He pulled at Marcus's shirt collar and yanked at Poppy's shoulder. They kept their eyes on the boy as they backed through the new opening in the wall. Moving swiftly into the dank space, the group put about a dozen feet between themselves and their attacker. "Come on."

The boy in the mask rose to his feet, his knees slightly bent as though he were about to pounce again.

"This way," Marcus whispered, turning to face the dim light in the elevator car. His vocal cords were raw.

"Everyone run!" said Dash. "Now!"

Dash and Poppy raced ahead of Marcus and Dylan. Dylan supported Marcus with his shoulder and helped him down the new corridor.

"Thank you," said Marcus.

"Just move!" said Dylan.

Marcus could hear the dog boy catching up quickly, but he kept the elevator's glow in the center of his vision. If there were walls around him, they were made of shadow. The house seemed to shiver, the floor rattling, the ceiling creaking, as if the passage were stretching longer and longer behind him. He hoped that whatever was happening would buy them a few extra seconds to get farther ahead of the kid in the dog mask.

Something flew from the darkness to the left of the elevator and collided with the group. Dash and Marcus shouted in surprise as Poppy and Dylan were spun around to face the direction from which they'd just come. Dazed, Marcus noticed that the boy in the dog mask was only several yards away, limping toward them determinedly.

"Poppy!" said an excited, high-pitched voice. "Oh my goodness!"

The *thing* that had barreled into them was Azumi. The glow from the elevator's lamp lit her panicked expression.

"Please help me!" Azumi glanced over her shoulder, looking back from where she'd come. "There's this crazy girl chasing me—"

"In here!" said Poppy, sliding the cage door open with a crash before stepping inside. "Quickly." The others followed. The space, which had seemed tight at first, expanded to fit everyone. The others huddled by the rear wall as Poppy shoved the handle. Accordion-like springs squealed their resistance, and the cage door closed.

A body smashed into the car from outside, rattling the brass gates. The old, cracking plastic of the dog mask pressed through the diamond-shaped holes in the cage. The boy reached inside, swinging his hands like claws in an arcade game, hoping to catch a prize.

Poppy knew it was only a matter of time before the boy grabbed the latch and swung the door open. Her mouth was dry. Her head felt like it was screwed on loosely. She understood she had to focus or she'd collapse. Staying to the side of the car, she looked for a panel of buttons that would send the elevator up or down. But there *were* no buttons. Instead, there was a circular apparatus marked with the word *OTIS* across the front, a small black knob sticking out of its top. "I don't know what to do," she whispered to herself. "*I don't know what to do!*"

"Get back or you're going to lose an arm when this thing moves," Dylan shouted, taunting the boy. Dash clung to his shoulder, shaking.

Azumi shouldered past them, pushing at the attacker's hands while dodging his violent swings. "Azumi, what are you doing?" Poppy asked. "Be careful!"

Marcus stayed pressed against the wall, rubbing his neck, wiping at his eyes, and clearing his throat. "Poppy! Make this thing move!"

"Okay, okay!" Poppy grabbed the black knob, sliding it to the right. To Poppy's surprise, the car lurched, its gears squealing sharply, and then the elevator began to rise.

The dog boy yanked his arms out of the cage and howled—a monstrous, inhuman sound coming from behind his mask—before disappearing into the shadows.

CHAPTER 24

WHEN THE FIRST floor was no longer in sight, Poppy swung the black knob back to the middle, and the car came to a screeching halt. They'd stopped between floors. For some reason, the walls of the elevator shaft weren't visible. Absolute darkness surrounded them, as if they were a vessel lost in outer space. The kids stumbled breathlessly into the center of the elevator, as if a hand might slip inside again and grab hold of them. Somehow, the car seemed even larger than it had been only seconds earlier.

At least they were away from danger. And even if they weren't, the new quiet felt like a balm for their bruises. They spent the next few seconds just breathing, checking their injuries. Each of them felt lucky to be alive.

Dylan was shattered. He was certain that if he hadn't mouthed off to the boy in the dog mask, none of his new friends would have been hurt. Even after all the conversations, after all the stories that the others had shared, he'd still half expected Del Larkspur to walk out from behind some curtain and tell them that it had all been a game. There would be cameras and lights and food and a comfortable place to read the rest of the film script, because that was how jobs always worked. People took care of you. *No one is coming*, he realized. *It's just you and Dash.* They'd been tricked.

He'd tried to push down the sense of terror he'd felt all day, starting with the white-hot panic after the strange flash on the stairs, and then again in the hallway with the boy in the bear mask. His mind whirled. If he was being honest, he'd had flashes of that same terror for weeks now, though he couldn't remember when it started, or why. Had it been in a dream? When he thought about the recent past, he couldn't place events into a simple time line. There were so many missing pieces, so many gaps. Deep down, he knew that Dash and his nightmares were spot on. It had taken something like this trip to open Dylan's eyes.

"Dylan, are you all right?" Dash put a hand on his brother's shoulder. "I'm so sorry."

Dylan felt so foolish he could only turn his head and try to hide his tears.

"Marcus, your neck," said Azumi, "let me take a look at it." Marcus shifted and everybody winced. There were several long ridges where the violin strings had bit into Marcus's skin. One of the marks was raw, oozing blood.

"I might have a Band-Aid," said Poppy, digging through her satchel. She pulled out a paperback—*The Lion, the Witch and the Wardrobe*—and flipped through a few pages, revealing several items that were placed inside. And just like that, she handed Marcus a Band-Aid. "You never know," she added. Her eyes lit up. "Oh, and this might help too." She reached again into her bag and grabbed something near the bottom. Opening her hand, she showed him a wrapped cherry cough drop.

"Thanks," Marcus whispered.

"Can I have one?" asked Dash, his own voice sounding raw. "That dog kid got me good too." Poppy nodded, and reached into her bag again. She frowned, pulled out the folder labeled *SPECIALS*, and laid it on the floor in the middle of the kids before reaching into her bag again for Dash's cough drop.

"Are *you* all right?" Dylan asked Azumi, who'd been watching them all with concern. "That girl who was chasing you—"

"She didn't hurt me," said Azumi. The others waited for her to go on. "I heard a voice calling to me, so I went to check it out. I got lost. Then . . . I thought I saw my sister—"

Marcus interrupted. "But isn't your sister—"

"Gone," said Azumi. "Yes, just like I told you, Marcus. I went after her anyway. When I got close, I saw that it wasn't Moriko. It was a girl wearing a chimpanzee mask. She growled at me!" Azumi flicked her long hair behind her shoulders, as if trying to compose herself. "She came at me, so I ran." She squinted at the file Poppy had placed on the floor before glancing at the group again. After a moment, she added, "So what do we do now?"

CHAPTER 25

DASH BENT DOWN and touched the folder. "What is this, Poppy?"

Poppy shook her head. "I grabbed it from the office before it . . . well, before it burned. I forgot I had it in my bag."

"*Specials?*" Dylan knelt beside his brother and flipped open the cover. "Whoa."

Inside, bundles of pages were divided into five groups, a large rubber band holding each group together.

Her heart skipping like mad, Poppy knelt by the twins. She spread the five bundles of paper out across the elevator's rug. A small black-and-white photograph was glued to the upper left side of each: portraits like mug shots of three boys and two girls. Poppy gasped. "I've seen these kids before," she said. "They were in the charcoal sketch I saw by the office door." She shot a self-conscious glance at Marcus. "Weeks ago, my Girl in the mirrors also gave me a sketch with them in it. They were standing in front of a stone wall, like the one near Larkspur's gate, wearing masks. Exactly like the masks we've seen in this house. I knew the Girl's drawing was a message when I first saw it, but I had no idea what it meant."

"This is too much." Azumi stood up and went over to the OTIS device. She placed her hand on the knob and said, "Up or down?"

The others stared at her, shocked.

Poppy shifted toward her. "I don't think we should be going anywhere right now."

"Marcus and Dash are hurt," said Azumi. "Shouldn't we, like, find a way out?"

"What do you think we've been trying to do?" asked Poppy. "For right now, we're safer in here than we were out there."

"We don't even know what *out there* is," said Azumi. She furrowed her brow and squeezed the knob tighter. Finally, she released an exaggerated sigh and joined the group again. "Fine."

Everyone focused on the folder again.

"So these have to be the kids who've been chasing us," said Dash. "Right?"

Poppy read the names in the files aloud. "Matilda Ribaldi, Randolph Hanson, Esme Alonso, Irving Wells, and Aloysius Mears."

"Aloysius! Poppy, that's the name we saw on the rabbit mask!"

"None of them look particularly *special*," said Dylan. "In fact, they all look pretty worn out."

He was right. Their eyes lacked the kind of spark or energy you usually saw in kids. Poppy had noticed the same in the sketch she'd found earlier hanging in the office. She'd noticed it in some of the kids at Thursday's Hope, especially when they first came in. And though something twisted inside her to admit it, she worried that she saw some of that same blankness in herself.

In the file photos, dark hollows marked the children's eyes, their mouths were downturned, and their postures were stiff, as if they were tensing against something awful to come. *It's like they're facing a firing squad*, she thought, then pushed the morbid thought away.

She removed the rubber band from the stack that belonged to the girl named Matilda and began sifting through it, reading bits and pieces of her life. "It says, 'Matilda is fond of story time, books, dolls, and singing nursery rhymes to herself. She is often shy and has to be coaxed to participate in any other group activities.'"

157

"We should read through the rest of these," said Dylan.

"There's no time!" said Azumi.

Dash scoffed. "We have nothing *but* time."

"Dylan's right," said Marcus. "If we can learn a little more about this house and the people who live—or lived—here, maybe we can figure a way out of this place."

"There are dozens of pages," said Azumi. "How are we supposed to get through all of this?"

Something echoed off in the distance—the sound of some small object hitting the ground from a great height. Everyone held their breath, waiting to hear another noise. But none came.

Poppy released a slow breath. "We have to try," she said, and then divided the stack and handed everyone a piece. "Five of them. Five of us. We work better when we work together."

CHAPTER 26

WHILE THE GROUP read, that same noise pinged out from the darkness every few minutes. It startled them each time. Thankfully, it didn't sound like it was getting any closer.

"Can I see your pages?" Dylan asked Dash, and he passed them over. After a moment, Dylan said, "Someone blacked out a whole bunch of the personal history sections in both the Irving and Aloysius files." The others nodded, showing him their files too. The papers were covered in thick markings.

"Maybe it was that Caldwell guy," said Dash. "The orphanage director." He glanced at his brother. Poppy noticed he was always looking over at Dylan, checking in with him. She envied such a close connection.

"That's what I'm hoping to find out," Poppy said.

Dash went on, scanning the sheets. "For some reason, the director didn't want anyone to know where the kids came from, or who they were before they got here."

"But there is a little bit about their personalities," said Marcus. "I think this whole folder was a small part of something larger. Look, there are notes throughout this one that show Cyrus must have kept more information about these kids . . ." As Marcus read more, his eyes grew wide. "And what he did to them," he added.

"What do you mean?" asked Poppy. "What did he do to them?"

"This kid, Randolph, was a musician." Marcus looked up at the others. "Just like me," he said slowly, pausing as if to absorb what that meant. "It says that Cyrus refused to let Randolph play his instruments. The boy in the dog mask attacked me with a broken violin. I think *he* was Randolph."

"Oh my goodness," said Poppy, holding her hand to her mouth as she read. "The director made Matilda destroy all of her dolls. They must have been the same dolls she tried to show me in the burning office."

Dash held up his pages. "Aloysius was mute. He had a sweet tooth. The director wrote that he contaminated Aloysius's favorite candies with a dye that stained his mouth and made him ill."

Dash looked sick himself. "I guess that was the black gunk I found inside the rabbit mask."

"'Irving loves being social and playing games,'" read Dylan. He cringed as he scanned what was on his page. "The director forced Irving to wear cuffs and chains around his ankles to stop him. Just like the kid I saw in the bear mask."

"What about your folder, Azumi?" asked Marcus. "What did you find?"

Azumi's face was frozen. When she spoke, her voice was tight and measured. "Esme missed her older sister," she said. Her eyes glinted with a flash of something dangerous, and for a moment, Poppy felt frightened to sit beside her. "Mr. Caldwell would not allow her to send letters. To respond at all. Even though she begged and begged and begged him. Esme was so angry, she wished she could . . ." Azumi glanced up, her vision clearing. "She must have been the one I saw in the ape mask."

After Poppy had heard all of this, she was nauseated. She couldn't imagine that this man—who shared her own last name—might possibly be related to her. The monster. "There's one thing no one's brought up yet," she said. The others watched her expectantly. "These pages were signed decades ago. If the kids who we encountered today are the same ones from this folder . . . well . . . you all know what that means, right?"

"You said earlier that you thought the house was haunted," Dylan answered slowly. "I guess we've found our ghosts."

"I don't understand," said Marcus. "How could someone be so horrible to a bunch of kids?"

"Because people can be horrible," said Poppy, her face like stone. "They don't need reasons."

"No wonder they're all so angry," said Dylan. "They've been hurt."

"*Hurt* is not the word I'd use," said Poppy. "It's way worse than that."

"Sorry if I don't have too much sympathy for them at this point," said Dash, and Azumi nodded emphatically. "Especially if they're the ones who brought us here."

"*Someone* contacted us," said Dylan.

"Can ghosts use the Internet?" asked Dash. "Can they mail letters?"

Dylan shrugged, looking off into the darkness surrounding them. "I don't know. It was just a thought."

"Let's say Dash is right," said Marcus. Dylan nudged his brother's shoulder playfully, and Dash managed a brief smile. Marcus cleared his throat and went on. "Let's say these orphans—"

"The Specials," said Dash.

"Right," said Marcus. "The Specials. Let's say they're the ones who wanted us to come to Larkspur." He paused, seeming lost in thought. "Why us? What's so special about us?"

"Well, Dash and me are kind of famous," said Dylan.

"Does that really make you special though?" asked Azumi, raising an eyebrow.

"Some people think so," Dash said.

"I'm still confused about the animal masks," said Poppy.

"The director wrote something about that too." Azumi sorted through Esme's file again. "Here it is." She read, "'The masks remove the children's identities. Whenever they glance in the mirror, they shall see nothing of their past. And whatever future they try to imagine shall be devoid of malignant expectation. These children will be my empty vessels. And I shall fill them with wonder.'" Azumi's laugh was dry as dust. "*Wonder,*" she spat, as if rejecting the word. "Mr. Caldwell had a pretty warped sense of it."

Poppy had been quiet, but she had been thinking hard. She frowned, turning the idea over again and again in her head. When she finally spoke, she wasn't loud, but what she said made the group sit up and listen. "What I think is more important is the connection that *we* have with the Specials."

"What do you mean?" asked Dylan.

"Five of them, five of us, right?" said Poppy. "There's Matilda and me. She loved her storybooks. And my books are my favorite treasure. Esme Alonso, the girl in the ape mask, was trying to reach out to her sister. And . . . and Azumi's sister went missing. That's another connection." Azumi squeezed her eyes shut in rejection. Poppy moved on. "Then there's you, Marcus, and Randolph Hanson. Both musicians. Both prodigies."

"What about *us*?" asked Dylan. "Am I supposed to be like the kid named Irving? The chained-up bear? What are you implying?"

"You *are* pretty charismatic," said Dash with a grin, peering over at Irving's paperwork. " 'Social, and friendly, and at times persuasive.' "

Poppy held back surprised laughter while Dylan glared at her. He turned to his brother with a smirk. "If that's the case, then *you're* the mute one."

Dash didn't take the bait. "Well, I don't talk that much, it's true."

Azumi's mouth was a flat line. "So we *are* like the Specials," she said.

"But what do they want with us?" asked Dash.

"Maybe they want us to take their places," said Dylan. "Maybe, like, if they trap us here, they can go free."

165

"We already *are* trapped," said Azumi. "And they haven't gone anywhere." She crossed her arms. "Maybe they want us dead."

Dash went gray and jumped to his feet. "DON'T SAY STUFF LIKE THAT!"

"Hey!" Dylan knocked his brother with his elbow, tossing a look that said *Chill*. Dash was still ashen, but he sat back down.

"We're lucky to have this folder," Dylan said. "Thanks, Poppy." He shuffled through the pages lying between them. Poppy blushed, squeezing her hands in her lap. "I don't think they expected us to get ahold of it," he added.

"Or maybe they did," said Azumi. "And it's filled with a bunch of lies." Everyone stared at her for a few seconds. "What? Did I say something funny?"

"There's something else we're missing," said Poppy, trying to sound upbeat. "Something that's not in this file. We haven't talked about how *we* are connected. The five of *us*."

"Sounds like you have another idea," said Marcus.

"Poppy's had a lot of good ideas, actually," said Dash. "If we stick with her, we might actually get out of this awful place."

Poppy felt herself flush red. She glanced around the group and realized that everyone was paying attention to her, as if she'd suddenly become their leader. This had never happened before, not in school, not at the group home, not anywhere.

"Spit it out, Poppy," said Azumi. "We don't have all day."

That same pinging sound echoed out from the darkness again. No one gave it a thought, until a few seconds later, when it was followed by another noise. A scraping, like something being dragged across the floor. And very, very close.

CHAPTER 27

EVERYONE LEAPT TO their feet and huddled in the center of the rug, crushing some of the file pages beneath them. They peered out anxiously through the bars of the cage, searching the ocean of black for movement.

"Someone's coming," whispered Azumi. "I *told* you."

The overhead lamp dimmed slightly. "No, no, no!" Poppy whimpered, and Dylan shushed her. She covered her mouth with a shaking hand.

There was movement in the distance, four figures emerging from the murk, closing in on them from every side of the elevator. The cage had never been a refuge. Instead, like a phosphorescent glow in the deepest depths, its lamp had created a lure. And now the predators had arrived. The scraping sounds got louder from all directions, as the figures marched slowly toward the elevator, a bull's-eye with an ever-shrinking circumference.

"Is it them?" asked Dash. "Is it the Specials?"

Marcus leaned forward and squinted, trying to make out the figures in the gloom. He snapped back into the middle of the huddle, as if for protection. "No," he said. "It's something else." The elevator lamp cast light only about a dozen feet from where they stood. And as the shapes came closer, their details were finally apparent.

"It's us," whispered Poppy, an echo of what Marcus had said in the game room hours earlier.

Approaching the cage were four papier-mâché figures like the ones that Azumi had pulled down from the mantel in the game room. But these dolls were as tall as the kids themselves. With their joints locked in place, the figures moved stiffly, swinging their weight from side to side, each of them dragging one foot and then the other in a syncopated rhythm.

There were the two identical figures painted light brown, dressed in shorts, graphic T-shirts, and sandals. Brothers. Around the corner from them, a girl painted pale pink hitched and swayed. Splotchy freckles covered her cheeks, and across her torso was the strap of a pink satchel. Adjacent to her was the boy with red hair. Around each of their necks hung thick white cords dragging along the floor behind them. Nooses.

The figures moved slowly, purposefully, sure of themselves, as if they knew they had all the time in the world.

"What do we do?" asked Dash in a strangled whisper

Dylan broke toward the OTIS device in the corner. "Up or down?" he asked.

"Up!" yelled Azumi.

"Down!" screamed Poppy at the same time.

Dylan tried to push the knob left, but the little sphere came off in his hand. The elevator didn't move. Panicked, Dash grasped at the end of the rod, but he only ended up cutting the tips of his fingers. The figures were within several feet. Poppy yanked the twins back into the center of the car, away from the walls of the cage.

Dash's whisper was practically inaudible now, as if he was mute with fear. "What do we do?" he repeated.

"Stay calm," said Poppy, thinking furiously. "I mean, these things are made out of paper. *Empty vessels*. Right? What could they possibly do to us?" But she had spoken too soon. The Poppy figure's right arm was severed below the elbow. Her words from the game room came back to haunt her. *You don't play with them. You break them.* From the hole in the plaster dangled an ashen arm, its fingers wiggling slightly.

As if reading Poppy's mind, Azumi said, "Those things aren't empty."

CHAPTER 28

MARCUS TURNED FROM the horror of the Poppy figure to end up face-to-face with his own, staring in at him from the other side of the brass bars. He steadied his feet, trying to find the lowest point of balance. Adrenaline spiked through him. He was going to have to fight.

The elevator was surrounded now, the figures pressed tight against the cage. The thing inside the Poppy figure raised its hand from the broken sleeve with a stifled groan and grabbed one of the bars.

The other figures began to groan too, twisting their limbs to crack out of the plaster, turning necks, bending elbows. Chunks of papier-mâché crumbled and fell to the floor.

The puppeteers were revealed. The Specials.

It was as Poppy had guessed. Matilda had come for Poppy, Randolph for Marcus, Irving for Dylan, and Aloysius and his black gash of a mouth had come for Dash. The cat, the dog, the bear, and the rabbit. Their eyes were empty pits.

For a few seconds, the masked orphans, the Specials, watched the group in stillness and silence. Dust coated their clothes and skin, clouds of it settling onto the black floor beneath them. Then, all at once, they attacked.

The bars of the cage clanged as the Specials threw themselves at them, screaming and shrieking. They yanked at the metal, banging their heads, whipping their arms and legs in a frenzy of movement.

Azumi, Poppy, Marcus, Dash, and Dylan clung to one another, some of them whimpering, some too stunned to make a sound. The metal around them began to squeal and cry as the brass bars bent under the pressure of the attack, making space for the Specials to reach farther inside. Clawlike fingers swiped at the group. Poppy screamed as Matilda got close enough to pull out a hank of her hair.

"They're going to tear us to pieces!" shouted Azumi. The others cringed in fear.

"That's not going to happen!" Poppy yelled. "We have to fight them! NOW!" And the kids inside the elevator broke apart.

173

Poppy and the twins flung themselves at their orphans, while Marcus spun away from the bars as the dog boy caught his jacket, and Azumi slipped quietly toward the elevator door.

"*You came,*" said Matilda's muffled voice as she swiped at Poppy's face. "*You actually came.*"

With the flat of her palm, Poppy smacked Matilda away from the wall of the cage. "I don't know you!" she shouted. Matilda laughed and swiped for Poppy again.

Aloysius and Irving tore at the twins' T-shirts, twisting the hems in their clenched fists.

Dash shoved himself into Aloysius's arm, pinning it against a bar. Irving released Dylan and grabbed for Dash, but Dash ducked away.

Out of reach of the orphans, Dash noticed Dylan's whole body stiffening. *He's going to have another attack!*

"DYLAN!" he yelled. He released Aloysius and jumped back, yanking his brother into the center of the cage.

Dylan snapped out of it. "What do you think you're doing?" he snarled.

Aloysius lunged, his hand coming perilously close to Dylan's face. Dash kicked out at him and then at Irving, who hissed and roared like the bear whose head he was wearing.

Marcus was struggling to rip his jacket away from Randolph's clutching fingers when he saw Azumi at the cage door, pulling frantically at the latch. "Azumi!" he shouted, yanking himself fiercely away from the dog boy. He flew across the cage, knocking her away. "What are you doing?!" he said. "You could let them in!"

Azumi blinked, as if coming out of a trance. She nodded. "We need to run."

"Run where?" he asked. "They're too fast. They'll catch us."

A noise above startled them. Randolph had leapt up above them, climbing up the bars of the elevator cage to the top. Marcus cowered in the center of the cage, covering his head and ducking to avoid Randolph's reach. Azumi jumped up and swiped at the boy, smacking his hand away. Randolph yowled, and Azumi shrieked, "Leave us alone, you nasty thing!"

Grabbing Poppy's bag, Matilda released a muted chuckle. She pulled herself violently backward, slamming Poppy's body into the cage. Poppy grunted and then straightened her shoulders to keep from tumbling out into the shadows. Clasping the bars, she struggled to stay upright.

All around her, the others were shouting, and Poppy wished she could help them. Everything was happening so fast. If it lasted much longer, the orphans would be inside the cage and Azumi's prediction would come true—the Specials would tear the group apart, as easily as Poppy had torn the arm off the papier-mâché doll. *There's got to be a way to escape this*, she thought, her brain spinning. *If we all huddle in the center of the cage . . . If we take them one at a time . . .*

But then Matilda got Poppy's hair in her hands again and jerked as hard as she could. Poppy screamed, feeling pinpricks of pain as follicles were torn from her scalp. Without thinking, Poppy reached through the bars and grabbed hold of the cat mask. She whipped herself backward, the mask still in her hands.

Matilda yelped and stumbled, holding her hands in front of her face. Poppy flung the mask to the floor of the elevator, steadying herself for the next round. But to Poppy's surprise, Matilda lowered her hands, revealing a shocked and horrified expression. Her icy eyes were frightened, her pale skin covered in patchy blotches of plaster.

The battle was still raging around them, but a stillness descended upon the two girls, something that Poppy was certain only they could feel. They stared into each other's eyes. Matilda's were blue and glistening. Seeing past the mask for the first time, Poppy felt a shock. There was a real girl inside, not just a monster. All of these orphans were *real kids*. Dead kids, probably, but real kids nonetheless. Poppy sensed a kind of desperation emanating from the girl, as if she expected that this respite would not last long.

It was then that Poppy realized the fighting had stopped. Turning, she noticed both groups were staring at her—the orphans and her friends.

The other three Specials, the ones still wearing masks, stepped away from the cage and toward Matilda.

"No!" said Matilda. The desperation on her face made Poppy sick. "Leave me alone. Leave me alone!" The three leapt upon Matilda, dragging her to the ground as she flailed and screamed, then huddled over her in a mass. *It looks like wolves feeding,* thought Poppy. She wanted to squeeze through the bars and help the poor girl, but she knew she couldn't take the time.

"Let's go!" said Poppy. She pushed through the group toward the elevator door. Unhooking the latch, she dragged the heavy accordion springs back slowly, slightly, opening a small gap. One by one, they all slipped out into the mysterious darkness that surrounded the cage.

They ran blindly for a while until Marcus stopped them. "Hold on. Where are we?"

"Yeah," said Azumi. "Poppy, which way should we go?"

Looking over her shoulder, Poppy could see the Specials rising from their spot on the floor. From their center, Matilda pushed her way out. She was wearing the cat mask once again. Poppy blinked. The mask that Poppy had torn from her face was still lying on the rug inside the elevator car. Where had this new mask come from?

A disturbing idea slithered into Poppy's skull: The mask had *grown* back.

Matilda darted forward. The others followed, backlit now by the elevator's lamp, making them into featureless hunters.

"It doesn't matter which way," said Poppy, grabbing Azumi by the hand. "Just run!"

CHAPTER 29

THEY SPRINTED THROUGH what seemed like endless dark.

They'd left the glow of the elevator's lamp, and Dash and Dylan were using their phones' flashlights to reveal the next few feet of floor, which sloped upward at a steep angle. As far as everyone could see, there were no walls, no furniture, nothing around them. It was as though the house had not yet dreamed up features for wherever they were headed.

Finally, Poppy stumbled over the edge of a rug and nearly shrieked with joy at seeing something familiar. With every step, more details of the house appeared around her, lit by the ghostly glow of the group's flashlights. There was a baseboard. The ceiling. An overturned wicker chair. A toy fire truck. Ahead, at the end of what was now a hallway, a closed door was rimmed with a halo of light.

Leaping to the front of the group, Poppy cried, "In here!" She swung the door inward, catching a glimpse of the space while everyone piled past her into the room. Then she shoved the door closed, turning the bolt to lock it.

Footfalls continued to ring out from the other side of the door, closer now, closer, followed by the moans and groans, screeches and rattling of the Specials, who were approaching faster than wildfire.

Stepping back to catch her breath, Poppy scanned the room. *Think, Poppy!* Thick curtains were drawn shut over several windows. Amber light emanated from two small crystal chandeliers that hung from the arched ceiling on opposite ends of the space—one in front of a wall of books, the other before a fireplace. In the corner were half a dozen musical instruments propped up on black metal stands. There were heavy chairs and tables just like she'd seen throughout the rest of the house scattered around the room.

If we can't find a way out of the house yet, we need to make a safe place inside it, she thought.

"We need to build a barricade," Poppy announced. She felt like Meg Murry from *A Wrinkle in Time*, saving her brother, Charles Wallace. "Bring anything heavy. And hurry!"

Marcus spun in place, carefully scanning what was available.

The twins practically attacked a substantial leather chair, dragging it to the door.

"Marcus!" Poppy called out as she made her way to a weighty desk. "Help me with this." She and Marcus shoved it up against the door. Azumi carried several piles of books as the twins went back for a small table made of dense wood. "Hand those to me," said Poppy, and then dropped the heavy books inside the desk drawers.

The twins' table wobbled as they lifted it atop the desk. Marcus grabbed a leg to keep it steady. "I've got it." Twisting it, the boys pushed it underneath the lip of the door frame.

"Give it a shove," said Dash.

Boom! Boom! Boom! The Specials had arrived. They began to pound on the door from the outside as the group stacked up everything in the room against it.

"Put that there," said Poppy as Azumi came lugging over a wide ceramic container with a potted palm sprouting from its center. The girls sat the plant on the leather chair's seat.

The pounding at the door grew stronger. The barricade shivered.

Azumi and Dylan stared at the barricade as if they could will it to hold. Marcus wandered into the corner of the room, examining the musical instruments Poppy had seen when she'd entered the space.

Poppy looked around again, wondering if there were any other doors that needed to be reinforced, checking all sides of the room, remembering what Dash had said earlier. *Poppy's had a lot of good ideas.* She blushed again. And that's when she noticed it—a large painting in a gilt frame. Almost four feet tall, it hung over the marble fireplace at the far end of the room, near the spot where the heavy desk had been. Poppy blinked, certain that her eyes were deceiving her, that her exhausted brain was playing tricks on her.

It was a portrait of a girl dressed in old-fashioned clothes and a flower pendant hanging from her neck. The painting's details were remarkably lifelike. But it wasn't the clothing or the skill of the artist that had captured Poppy's attention—it was the girl herself. Wide golden eyes. Pale skin that made the girl's brown hair, which was pulled behind her ears, even darker by contrast.

No longer trapped in a mirror, the Girl was staring at Poppy once more.

This was *her* Girl.

She seemed to watch as Poppy approached.

A small brass plaque had been screwed into the metal at the bottom of the frame. Engraved there was a name: *Consolida*

Caldwell—Beloved Daughter and Sister. When Poppy read it, she released a yelp that sounded around the room.

A hand grasped her shoulder, and Poppy jumped. Turning, she found Dash standing behind her. "What is it?" he whispered.

She pointed at the plaque at the bottom of the frame. "This is the Girl. My *Girl*. From the mirrors."

"She has your name too?"

Poppy nodded.

Dash stepped closer to the fireplace mantel. "The painting is signed by someone named Frederick Caldwell. Who's he?"

"Her father? Her brother? I don't—" *Boom! Boom! Boom!* The pounding at the door rose in volume and strength, shaking the room.

Dash stared at Poppy in desperation, as if her answer would save them from all the trouble they were in. But she didn't have any ideas.

"I don't know!" Poppy cried. "All I know is that if we don't find somewhere safe to hide, and soon, I might actually lose it." Her bottom lip began to tremble, and she bit down on it until it hurt.

CHAPTER 30

SOMETHING ABOUT THE instruments in the corner had mesmerized Marcus, and it wasn't just the idea that he'd finally located an actual "music room" in this mad place. Somewhere far away, the Musician's melody, "Larkspur's Theme," began to echo again.

Boom! Boom! Boom! The furniture at the door shivered slightly. Marcus knew he needed to do something to help everyone here. And quickly.

The last time he'd felt safe had been in the ballroom while playing the piano. The music had provided that serenity. It had protected him, a barrier to keep bad things away.

Marcus couldn't decide what instrument to pick up first. There was a delicate violin, an antique cello, a guitar, a harp, an oboe. And finally, sitting against the wall of bookshelves was a baby grand piano, the twin of the one he'd played downstairs. Its lid was raised, its strings gleaming in the light that fell from the chandeliers.

The tune in his head grew louder, as if the Musician were begging Marcus to let it out. The ivory pieces almost grinned at him as he sat down at the bench. Then, inhaling sharply, Marcus began to play.

The banging at the door faded to a rattle. Poppy, Dash, and Dylan turned to look at him, while Azumi continued to hold herself against the barricade, as if it would break without her help.

Finally, Marcus had an audience. And he found that he liked it.

"Marcus," said Dash, "whatever you're doing, it's working."

"It's the same song you were playing when we found you in the ballroom downstairs," said Poppy quietly. "It's like a . . . a spell." Marcus closed his eyes, remembering how he'd sneered at Poppy when she'd mentioned the girl she'd seen in her mirrors. Was the Musician's tune really so different from Poppy's visions? Of course it wasn't. And now Marcus couldn't look at Poppy without wishing he could take everything back.

As the music echoed off the walls and high ceiling, Marcus found himself surrounded by memories again. Visions of happy family dinners. His oldest brother Isaac's tearful apologies for messing with his instruments. Finding time alone in the house after school to rehearse without worrying about his mother's response. He felt safe. He felt like he was home. And he knew the others could feel it too.

CHAPTER 31

BLOOD WAS RUSHING through Dash's head. The room seemed to throb with the rhythm of his heartbeat, like an echo of the banging that had disappeared from behind the door, and his skin felt like it was on fire. Poppy stood with Azumi at the other end of the barricade, transfixed by Marcus's melody, oblivious to Dash's sudden affliction. Something was wrong—*more wrong* even than being trapped in this insane building.

Dylan was right beside him, staring into nothing, but Dash suddenly felt like they were miles apart from each other. He blinked, and the past rushed at him. A memory as vivid as a dream.

The dressing room is dark. Dylan is at the door, soaking wet, reaching for the lamp. Everything is about to change, and it's going to be my fault.

I'm so sorry, Dylan. I'm so, so sorry.

Dash shook the images away. Coming back into himself, he took his brother's elbow. But Dylan didn't seem to notice. After a moment, Dash shook his brother's arm. Still nothing. "Dylan?" he asked. "Are you okay?" When Dylan still didn't answer, Dash turned him like a rag doll so they were face-to-face.

But Dylan wasn't there. His eyes were blank, his jaw slack. And then Dash knew—whatever Marcus's music was doing to this room, whatever protection the tune was offering, whatever it was that had driven away the Specials, was affecting Dylan too. But how? Why?

"Dylan! Dylan, can you hear me?"

Dylan's eyes focused slightly, zeroing in on Dash's face. Then tears welled up on his lower lids.

"What's wrong?" asked Dash. "What is it?"

Dylan opened his mouth as if to say something. "You . . . you . . ." Saliva clicked in the back of his throat. "You . . . were . . . there . . ."

Dylan's mouth went wide in a silent scream.

Opening his eyes, Marcus blinked away tears and looked down at his hands, still moving across the keys, hammers hitting the strings that vibrated the air around him. Sounds of a scuffle came from the doorway, but he knew he had to focus on the music.

To his surprise, Marcus heard another instrument chime in—the high hum of a violin beginning to accompany the piano. At first Marcus thought it was only in his head, but then he glanced across the room; the violin was hovering in the air, its bow slowly sliding across the strings. Marcus nearly fell off the bench, but he steadied himself, not daring to pause, hoping that his momentary break in concentration wouldn't end whatever enchantment seemed to have blessed this space. The atmosphere around the violin shimmered, as if someone invisible to ordinary human perception was standing there playing it. The violin's high voice swooped and swirled, not *matching* the tune of the piano but adding something to it that made the melody even more hypnotic and lovely. Soon, it was joined by several other instruments. Marcus watched in awe as the guitar leaned forward and began to play by itself, followed by the cello and the flute.

The music swelled as a boy materialized, the conductor of this magical orchestration. He glanced at Marcus and then turned back to the instruments. He lifted his hands and the instruments almost seemed to nod at him. Marcus recognized the boy's red curls, his deep brown eyes. It was his uncle, Shane.

It was the Musician. Of course. He felt a surge of love for this person, whom he'd never met and yet had always known. They didn't need to speak. This music was their conversation. It always had been.

"Marcus!" Poppy called out from across the room. Was she kneeling on the floor beside Azumi? *Who is that?*

"Don't worry," said Marcus, raising his voice over the music. "He's a friend."

CHAPTER 32

THOUGH POPPY WAS worried about Azumi, who was looking blankly on the floor at her knees, she couldn't peel her gaze away from the strange figure that had appeared by the piano—a redheaded boy who looked, if not exactly like Marcus, then at least like a close relation. Where had he come from?

Poppy shook her head. She felt the same sense she'd gotten whenever she'd seen the Girl in the mirror. Marcus looked happy to be playing with him, as if he'd known this boy for a long, long time.

He'd called her crazy.

Crazy!

He must have known she was telling the truth about the Girl. He'd *known*, but he'd still made her feel . . . wrong. Wrong about herself. Wrong about her own story.

A flash of rage rushed over Poppy's skin, a hot wave that pushed away the chill of fear in the house. She wanted to rush across the room and knock Marcus from the bench, throttle him. But before she could even move, she heard a deep rumble of laughter. She looked around for a moment before realizing that the laughter had come from inside her head.

Poppy knew: Something very bad was about to happen.

CHAPTER 33

THERE WAS A loud crack, and the piano trembled. Marcus nearly jumped out of his skin. He forced himself to continue playing, but several of the piano keys went mute. Peering into the body of the instrument, he could see snapped strings, their hammers hitting only air.

His uncle's tune was suddenly missing part of its register, and to Marcus, it was as jarring as if he'd just witnessed someone lose a limb.

One by one, the silver keys of the flute snapped away from the body, clattering to the floor until it could only yelp out a flat whistle.

Shane vanished, and Marcus screamed. "No!"

There was another shocking *SPROING* as eight more of

the piano's strings broke, silencing another octave, weakening the strength of the melody.

From a few feet away, there came a shattering smash. The string section of the concerto was eradicated. The violin and the guitar lay on the floor in wooden slivers, as if they'd exploded.

A wave of nausea swelled from Marcus's stomach and knocked at the top of his head. That feeling of safety that had come from his uncle's music was quickly disappearing. Something in the house, in the room, was determined to send the music away, to stop the good memories, to *frighten* him. He closed his eyes, trying to picture his uncle's face again, but all he could see now was black.

Across from the piano, the shimmering spots that had surrounded the instruments were disappearing, replaced now by the oddly visible notion of stillness and quiet.

The only instrument that continued to accompany him was the cello—its melody began to stretch and strain, losing pitch, as though someone were wrenching the tuning brackets this way and that. Then, with a finality that was almost painful, the last strings on the piano and cello snapped. All that was left of the music now was a distorted echo.

Movement by the portrait of Poppy's girl caught his eye. Dirt and dust fell from the chimney.

Poppy and Dash were staring at the instruments from the barricade by the door. Azumi was lying on the floor, lifting her head as if coming back to consciousness. And Dylan stood wide-eyed, frozen, as if in shock.

Then two figures dropped from the chimney. Dust dissipated as the figures slowly stood up, revealing their masks. The music had stopped, and the dog and the cat had found their way in.

CHAPTER 34

"WHERE AM I?" Azumi asked, color returning to her cheeks.

"You fainted," said Poppy. "You'll be okay. We just have to move away from here. Like, now."

"What's going on?" Azumi turned to see Matilda and Randolph stepping slowly away from the fireplace, toward the group.

Dash helped her to her feet. The trio gathered around Dylan and then backed away from the intruders, staying along the wall for safety.

Poppy's mind rushed through the events of the past hour. Back at the elevator, Matilda had been lucid for a moment, as if she'd regained her sense of self. *Maybe*, Poppy thought, *if I talk to her now, she'll answer me.*

"Matilda—" she began, but the girl in the cat mask threw back her head and shrieked, as if hearing that name pierced her like an ice pick through the forehead.

The group hurried away from the two orphans, quickly meeting Marcus at the wall of bookshelves at the opposite end of the room.

Poppy squeezed her eyes shut, trying to reason out what exactly had happened in the elevator. *You came*, Matilda had said. *You actually came.* There was a tussle and then . . . Poppy had yanked off the stupid cat mask.

That was it. The mask! The orphanage director had written it himself in the *SPECIALS* file: *The masks remove the children's identities.* What if they only needed to recognize one another, to share their true selves? To forge a connection, like Poppy had done with her Girl whenever she'd looked in mirrors?

Poppy blinked.

The Specials were now only a few strides from the group. Randolph, the dog, the music prodigy, carried his smashed violin. He dragged its battered body along the ground behind him, where it bounced and skittered, its strings squealing as they twisted and rubbed against one another. Matilda, the cat, held one of her ruined dolls by its matted hair, as if she intended to bludgeon someone with it.

The pounding noise at the barricaded door started up again. Now that the house, or *something*, had stopped Marcus's music from playing, the other orphans had returned.

"We have to take off their masks!" yelled Poppy.

Dylan pressed his head firmly against the stacks of shelves behind him, gasping for breath.

The two Specials lunged forward.

CHAPTER 35

THE GIRL IN the cat mask came at Dash, scratching at his arms, his neck, his torso. He howled at her cold, sharp touch, trying to bat her away, but she was too strong. "Help!" he called out to Dylan, but Dylan was still weak from whatever had happened to him by the doorway.

A trilling of notes sounded nearby, shocking everyone out of the struggle.

Turning, Dash saw that Marcus was beside him, blowing into a harmonica—*Where did Marcus get a harmonica?*—performing the same tune that he and the ghostly young conductor had played several minutes ago.

The orphans began backing away from the group. They held their hands to their ears, as if this new noise was painful to them.

This song filled Dash with a sense of warmth and calm, but Dylan was squirming, as if in discomfort. Azumi sat hunched over him. Was she trying to help him somehow? "Dylan, what's wrong?" Dash screamed.

"Now!" said Poppy at the same time. "Grab them!" She leapt toward the masked pair.

Poppy flailed with Matilda, their arms locked around each other's necks. "Dash! Please! Help me!" Poppy's fingers strained toward the edge of the cat mask. Randolph sprang toward them.

Adrenaline flashed through Dash's system. He leapt to his feet, taking the dog boy by surprise. "Got you!" he yelled, and ripped off the mask.

Everything stopped. Slowed. Even the dust went still. It was as if the entire house was listening to the drawl of Marcus's harmonica. Matilda and Randolph's masks were on the ground, torn.

Matilda and Randolph straightened, their jaws slack in disbelief. Their eyes were wide with hope and fear, glistening with what Dash could only think of as *life*.

Holding his breath, he brought his attention back to Dylan, who'd gone blank again. There was something he knew he needed to do.

You ... were ... there ...

Dash reached out to wipe away his brother's tears, but Dylan released an unearthly howl, and Dash was shocked into stillness. Then the room went dark.

CHAPTER 36

FLASH.

You . . . were . . . there . . .

Dash is hiding in Dylan's dressing room on the set of *Dad's So Clueless*. It's dark. The lamp on the table beside Dylan's favorite chair sparked when Dash tried to turn it on, so he left it alone. The only light is coming from a crack in the door where Dash has left it slightly ajar. Dash has placed a bucket of water on top of the door—a trick—to get back at Dylan for all the cruel tricks he's played on the cast and the crew of the show over the years. When Dylan opens the door, the water will spill down, soaking him, shocking him, making him scream. Dash will jump out and laugh, and yeah, Dylan will be mad, but he deserves it. Maybe after this, Dylan will learn his lesson, and Dash will stop getting blamed for his brother's mischief.

Footsteps approach, and Dash covers his mouth to hold back a snicker. The door opens and the bucket tips. Water splashes. Dylan shouts: *What the . . . ?* But then the bucket falls. It hits Dylan's skull with a solid *THUNK*.

That wasn't supposed to happen.

Oww, says Dylan, stumbling into the dark room. He clutches his head as he staggers toward the lamp—the same lamp that sparked when Dash had tried to turn it on minutes earlier.

Dash sees what is about to happen. He leaps out from his hiding place, screaming for his brother to *Stop! Wait! Don't move!*

But Dylan is confused. He's dripping wet with water and blood. He touches the lamp's switch.

White light fills the room—flashes like paparazzi taking pictures at a Hollywood premiere. Dash screams as Dylan's body stiffens, and an electric buzzing blasts the room.

Flash.

You . . . were . . . there . . .

At the emergency room, his parents give Dash the bad news. "It was an accident," they say. "It wasn't your fault."

But Dash refuses to listen. How can Dylan be *dead* when they're still giggling in the backseat on the way home from the hospital? When they're already home, playing hide-and-seek together? When they're whispering secrets to each other late into the night?

Dash thinks it's a cruel way to punish him for what he

did—his parents trying to make Dash believe that he electro-cuted his own brother. He already feels terrible about the trick.

But maybe Dash deserves it. A little bit. At least when Dylan played his tricks, no one ever got seriously hurt.

Flash.

You . . . are . . . here . . .

But I am not.

"We're going to need you downstairs in fifteen," says the bouncy brunette, whose name neither boy can remember. "Just a heads up. 'Kay?"

She isn't a producer, Dash realizes. In her white coat, he can see that she's a nurse. Or a doctor. And she's not just playing one on TV.

"Downstairs?" asks Dylan with a smirk. "For what? Are we shooting the next scene?" The producer raises an eyebrow and continues to look at Dash, as if only his reply matters. Dylan waves at her, trying to get her attention. "Uh, hello? Am I invisible or something?"

Or something.

"She completely ignored me," says Dylan.

But of course she did, Dash understands now. Everyone does. Dylan is not the patient. Dash is. This is not the set of *Dad's So Clueless.* It is a hospital. A real hospital where they are struggling to make Dash see the truth.

The truth.

He remembers now. His parents admitted him after they found him wandering far from home one night, when he was insisting that Dylan was out there and needed his help. But that had been *after* Dylan's funeral. A funeral that, to Dash, is still only a vague recollection.

The doctors insist on keeping an eye on him. Dash has been seeing things. Seeing his deceased brother. He's been carrying a guilt so powerful, Dash thinks now, that it has managed to raise the dead.

There are emails and texts and cards from the cast and the crew, but no one is allowed to visit. Dash is a special case. He needs special care. He knows he won't be returning to the set again.

Did they write Scooter off the show? Was it Dylan's fault for always being so difficult? Or was it what Dash had done?

Nothing makes sense anymore.

Nothing, that is, until the email from Larkspur Productions, LLC, arrives. The email from Del.

Dylan! Dash! . . . What's up?

Dash yanked himself away from Dylan, as if a static shock had jerked him awake after a long, long night of dreaming.

CHAPTER 37

DYLAN TURNED AWAY, unable to look at his twin any longer.

"How long have you known?" asked Dash, still hearing music in the background. It sounded like a faint memory.

"Just now," said Dylan, his voice tired. "Before, I had glimpses. But now, with this music, and the house, and . . . I've seen everything." Dash tried to take Dylan's hand, but Dylan flinched away from him.

The girl, Matilda, was staring into Dylan's eyes. Her gaze was piercing, almost painful. She knew too. She knew everything.

Poppy faced the twins, confused. "How long have you known what?" she asked.

Dylan ignored her, looking into Matilda's sad blue eyes

instead. "I can't say," he said. Dash hung his head, breathless. "I don't know how. I don't . . ."

Matilda nodded, cradling the doll in her arms. "You will," she said. Her voice was singsong, almost motherly, as if the girl had long practiced this character with her dolls. "You'll do it together."

Suddenly Matilda's face crumpled as if she'd been stabbed in the stomach. She bent over, moaning. "He won't let us go." Matilda glanced up, her gaze settling on each of them. "And he won't let you go either." Her voice started to fade.

"Who won't let you go?" said Poppy. "Do you mean Cyrus? Cyrus Caldwell? The man who hurt you?"

But Matilda covered her face with her hands, too pained to answer.

Marcus was still playing his harmonica, and Randolph stepped toward him. Marcus backed away, but Randolph dropped the broken violin on the ground. He listened to Marcus's song, breathing it deeply as if it were oxygen.

Marcus stopped. The silence was so jarring that everyone jumped. "They took away your music," he said to Randolph. "Here. This is yours now." He wiped the instrument off on his shirt and then held it out to the boy. Randolph's eyes lit up, like a kid at a birthday party. "Go on. Take it. Play."

Randolph grasped the harmonica, holding it up to the light, looking as though he'd never seen one before. He placed it against his lips and blew tentatively. Within seconds, he was mimicking Marcus's tune. The notes danced around the room, surrounding them with the sensation of shelter from a storm.

Something strange was happening to Randolph. As he played, his joy coursing through the air, his body began to change. To lose color.

Randolph was fading, Marcus realized. He could look right through him, at Dylan's astonished expression.

Then the boy who'd attacked them simply went away, taking the happy tune with him.

"Randy?" Matilda asked. Now she sounded like the little girl that she was—or that she once had been. She tilted her chin as if sensing something the rest of them could not. Then she flinched, grasping her stomach again, and doubled over. She dropped her ruined doll, and it hit the floor with a soft *thud*. Poppy hurried over but Matilda stepped back, not wanting to be touched.

"What happened?" Dash asked.

"Marcus gave him back what Cyrus took away from him," said Dylan, his voice flat. "His music."

"We can help you too!" Poppy said to Matilda.

"Yes," said Azumi, breathless. "What is it that *you* need?"

"No . . . time," the girl whispered. Already, her face was shifting, beginning to resemble the mask that Poppy had ripped away from her only minutes earlier. Matilda ran across the music room and tore into the barricade.

"Wait!" Poppy took several hesitant steps after her. "They might still be out there."

But Matilda wasn't listening. As soon as she'd cleared enough room, she slipped out into the hallway and was gone.

For several seconds, the group waited in horrified silence for the masked orphans to come piling through the doorway. But soon, they realized that the Specials had vanished, leaving Poppy, Marcus, Dylan, Dash, and Azumi alone with one another.

"Is it safe?" asked Azumi, finally rising to her feet.

Marcus continued to look at the gap in the doorway. "For now, maybe. I hope."

"Do you think if we do the same for the others," said Poppy, "if we help Esme, and Irving, and Aloysius, and Matilda . . . if we give them what the director took from them . . . do you think they'll be free, like Randolph?"

"Maybe," said Dash. Eyes closed, he added, as if desperate, "Maybe once we do that, the house will release us too."

Just then, Dylan shouted, unable to control himself. He fell to his knees and screamed out what sounded like the last of the life that was still inside him.

CHAPTER 38

DYLAN HAULED HIMSELF to his feet and streaked toward the door!

"Dylan, stop!" Dash cried out after him. "Wait!" But he stayed where he stood, as if frightened to actually approach.

At the door, Dylan turned. "No! I don't want your help. Your *help* is what got me into this mess in the first place." His expression twisted, as if he were fighting to keep an angry beast pinned down somewhere deep inside himself. "I guess we do actually get to play our own roles from now on, little brother."

Dash's face crumpled. "You can't leave."

Dylan sneered, heaving breath. "Apparently, none of us can! And maybe some of us *don't deserve to*. So what difference does it make?" He swiveled his shoulders and, like a sigh, slipped out into the hallway and disappeared into the darkness.

Dash stared at the others, stunned. "You can't leave *me*," he whispered, as if to himself. "That's what I meant."

"You asked him *how long he's known*," said Poppy. "What did you mean?"

"There was an accident." Dash looked up. He chewed his bottom lip for a few seconds. "On the set of our show. Dylan . . . He . . . He was killed. It was my fault. I was trying to teach him a lesson."

Azumi stared. "What are you talking about? He was just here."

Marcus shoved his hands in his pockets. "No! You're saying . . . What are you saying?"

"He's saying that his brother is a ghost," Poppy answered carefully. "A spirit. Whatever you want to call it. *Him*. I'm sorry, Dash."

"A ghost?" Two blooms of color appeared on Marcus's parchment-white cheeks. "Dylan?"

"Yeah," said Poppy. "Kinda like that boy who appeared next to your piano. The one who looked just like you." She glared at him. "After everything that just happened, you're really going to question this?"

Marcus shuddered. "Today it's like I've been going crazy, but I know I'm not crazy. What I've seen is real."

"Interesting," said Poppy. "*How do you think that feels?*"

"*Crazy*," Dash whispered. "I remember now. I was in a

hospital. I kept talking to everyone about Dylan like he was alive. No one believed that he was right there beside me. No one could hear him or see him like I could. It was like I thought they were all teasing us by ignoring him. When we got that email from Del, we snuck out together. Went home. Found Dylan's secret piggy bank. I knew he'd been stealing from the cast and crew for years. But I had no idea how much he'd collected. We took a cab to the airport and bought two tickets. Nobody said a word to me about the empty seat, the one I'd paid for. They must have thought I was . . . Well . . . I don't know what they thought. But in this house, things were different. You could see him too."

"I remember now," said Poppy, her jaw dropping. "I'd read about the accident online. I'd heard one of you was hurt. But I didn't realize—"

"You guys must think I'm so stupid," said Dash, wiping furiously at the tears streaming down his face.

"No one thinks you're stupid," said Azumi. "Our minds can be the worst kind of tricksters. Especially when bad things happen. And bad things *do* happen. They'll keep happening too. As long as we're here." She looked back at the busted piano. "When Marcus's music was playing, all I could think of was my sister."

The four who were left in the music room didn't know what else to say or do. Marcus tried to squeeze Dash's shoulder, but Dash only shook him off. Poppy and Azumi found themselves holding hands. It took several long seconds for Poppy to gather herself. She went over to the door and closed it again, then shoved some of the furniture back into place.

"So when we were downstairs, you lied," Poppy said to Marcus in a low voice. "When I told you my story about the Girl in the mirrors"—she glanced at the portrait hanging over the fireplace—"you said that I was *crazy*. But you had experienced the same thing. Why would you do that?"

"You're right," Marcus answered softly. "He . . . the Musician's always been with me. I think he's my uncle. I should have told you, but I was scared. I'm sorry."

Poppy's eyes flashed. She exhaled and regrouped, her mind churning. After a few seconds, she added, "At least we know now what we all have in common."

"And what's that?" asked Azumi.

"We've all been haunted," said Poppy. "In our own way. Maybe that's the real reason we're here. Maybe that's how this place, or the spirits inside it, were able to find us."

"To lure us," Marcus added.

Azumi nodded. "To trap us."

"Or at least to try," said Poppy. "We know now that we're different. But I think whatever lives here underestimates us."

"Maybe not," said Dash. "Maybe the evil inside this place knows exactly what it's doing."

Quiet filled the room for a moment, like a held breath.

"We'll go find your brother when you're ready, Dash," Poppy said. "And then we're getting out of here. Now that we have a better idea of how. We're getting out of here together." A flicker of motion captured her attention, as if the portrait of the Girl had caught fire, but looking once more at the painting over the fireplace, nothing had changed. Or had it? Poppy noticed Consolida Caldwell—beloved daughter and sister—smiling at her. Had the Girl been smiling before?

When Poppy turned back to the group, Marcus and Azumi stared at her as if they expected her to spout out all the answers they needed to hear. Dash hung his head, tears dripping silently from the tip of his nose.

Poppy didn't have any answers. She knew that none of them did. What they did have was one another. And maybe that was enough to keep them going, to keep them strong, until they could find their way out of this nightmare. Poppy wanted to believe that more than anything. She really did.

Making her way to the other three, Poppy held out her arms and gathered everyone together. And for the first time in a long time, she felt safe.

From all corners of the room, there came a series of creaks and cracking sounds, as if the house were settling into the earth, satisfied.

ART CREDITS

INSIDE FRONT COVER
Photos ©: paper: Scholastic Inc.; fire: CG Textures

INTERIOR
Photos ©: 4: Illustration by Ben Perini for Scholastic Inc. based on masks by CSA Plastock/Getty Images; 25: main: Lewis W. Hines/Library of Congress; feet and sheet: Keirsten Geise for Scholastic Inc.; 46–47: mansion: Dariush M/Shutterstock, Inc.; fog: Maxim van Asseldonk/Shutterstock, Inc.; clouds: Aon_Skynotlimit/ Shutterstock, Inc.; moon: Mykola Mazuryk/Shutterstock, Inc.; composite: Shane Rebenschied for Scholastic Inc.; 57: rabbit mask: CSA Plastock/Getty Images; boy: Fancy/Media Bakery; staircase: Anna Bogush/Shutterstock, Inc.; lollipop: Hayati Kayhan/Shutterstock, Inc.; 72: background: Ppictures/Shutterstock, Inc.; bingo machine: Jonathan Kitchen/Getty Images; bingo balls: GeoffBlack/Getty Images; 106: standing doll: ejay111/Getty Images; clear-eyed doll: Prachaya Roekdeethaweesab/Shutterstock, Inc.; burnt head: AAR Studio/Shutterstock, Inc.; torso doll: mofles/Getty Images; clothed doll: Perfect Lazybones/Shutterstock, Inc.; wall and floor: Lora liu/Shutterstock, Inc.; 138: paper: Scholastic Inc.; floor: CG Textures; 145: hallway: Peter Dedeurwaerder/Shutterstock, Inc.; violin: AtomStudios/Getty Images; pants: michaeljung/Shutterstock, Inc.; boy: Keirsten Geise for Scholastic Inc.; dog mask: CSA Plastock/Getty Images; 158: girl photo: Larry Rostant; pen: Scholastic Inc.; paper/folders/rubberband/scratches: Scholastic Inc.; scissors: Photodisc; wood texture: CG Textures; 171 background: phoelix/Shutterstock, Inc.; gate: Songpan Janthong/Shutterstock, Inc.; left arm: Khakimullin Aleksandr/Shutterstock, Inc.; doll top: Faded Beauty/Shutterstock, Inc.; doll bottom: Jeff Wilber/Shutterstock, Inc.; wig: exopixel/Shutterstock, Inc.; 190: room: Library of Congress; cello: DK Arts/Shutterstock, Inc.; 216 girl: roban-gel69/Fotolia; frame: Chatchawan/Shutterstock, Inc.; mantle: Zick Svift/ Shutterstock, Inc.; wallpaper: Larysa Kryvoviaz/Shutterstock, Inc.; 218–219: mansion: Dariush M/Shutterstock, Inc.; fog: Maxim van Asseldonk/Shutterstock, Inc.; clouds: Aon_Skynotlimit/Shutterstock, Inc.; composite: Shane Rebenschied

Enter Shadow House

Each image in the
book reveals a
haunting in the app.

Search out hidden
sigils ▽ in the book
for bonus scenes in
the app.

Step into ghost stories,
where the choices you make
determine your fate.

CAN YOU ESCAPE?

. . . if you dare.

Navigate your way through chilling ghost stories.

Share scares on the Shadow House message boards.

Come play with us.

About the Author

Dan Poblocki is the author of several books for young readers, including *The House on Stone's Throw Island*, *The Book of Bad Things*, *The Nightmarys*, *The Stone Child*, and the Mysterious Four series. His recent novels, *The Ghost of Graylock* and *The Haunting of Gabriel Ashe*, were both Junior Library Guild selections and made the American Library Association's Best Fiction for Young Adults list in 2013 and 2014. Dan lives in Brooklyn, in an apartment with walls that happily do not move around while he's writing. Visit him online at www.danpoblocki.com.